RANGE TRAMP

D. B. Newton

THORNDIKE
CHIVERS

This Large Print edition is published by Thorndike Press®, Waterville, Maine USA and by BBC Audiobooks Ltd, Bath, England.

Published in 2005 in the U.S. by arrangement with Golden West Literary Agency.

Published in 2006 in the U.K. by arrangement with Golden West Literary Agency.

U.S.   Hardcover 0-7862-7961-3   (Western)
U.K.   Hardcover 1-4056-3579-7   (Chivers Large Print)
U.K.   Softcover   1-4056-3580-0   (Camden Large Print)

The text of this Large Print edition is unabridged.
Other aspects of the book may vary from the original edition.

Set in 16 pt. Plantin by Ramona Watson.

Printed in the United States on permanent paper.

British Library Cataloguing-in-Publication Data available

Library of Congress Cataloging-in-Publication Data

Newton, D. B. (Dwight Bennett), 1916–
    Range tramp / by D.B. Newton.
       p. cm. — (Thorndike Press large print Westerns)
    ISBN 0-7862-7961-3 (lg. print : hc : alk. paper)
    1. Large type books.   I. Title.   II. Thorndike Press large print Western series.
PS3527.E9178R36 2005
    813'.52—dc22   2005015302

RANGE TRAMP

Chapter 1

Bannister hadn't reckoned on a toll gate. The twists of this wagon road, snaking down from the high pass he had crossed at dawn, brought it into sight without any warning at all. In his surprise, the startled jerk of the hand that held the reins reached the dun horse and briefly halted it; he swore softly and sent it on again with the quick touch of a spur, hoping the moment's hesitation hadn't been noticeable.

You never knew who might be watching.

Beyond the closed gate, set into a peeled-pole fence that was anchored in the rocks that enclosed this narrow gap through which he traveled, he saw buildings — chiefly, a good-sized, two-storied log structure with a steep shake roof, and a barn that had a corral beside it. A flume of hollowed half-logs channeled runoff from a spring. A small meadow fronted the buildings, while behind them the mountain rose in steps that were black with timber, and broken by granite faces, to be lost finally in a sea of mist.

Even in early June, the air held the bite of high country chill. Blue smoke lifted lazily from the chimney of the main building. That, and a couple of horses moving in the corral, were the only signs of life.

Jim Bannister's glance kept busy beneath the brim of his pulled-down hat. As he moved ahead, it might have been an accident that kept his hand within inches of the gun strapped at his waist, or the skirt of his unbuttoned windbreaker pushed back out of the way, behind the jut of the wooden handle. He was still a little distance from the gate, still not changing his unhurried pace, when a man appeared from somewhere and came forward to meet him.

This was a gaunt figure, in a fur cap and a red-checked mackinaw — Bannister could not tell if there might be a gun underneath his coat. The contours of his face, with its few straggles of white whiskers, were distorted by the wad of tobacco tucked into one leathery cheek. The man waited on the other side of the fence as the stranger approached, and made no answer to his brief nod.

Bannister indicated the crudely lettered sign nailed to a post beside the gate:

"Horse and rider, $2" it said. "Wagons $3." He suggested, "A little steep?"

"You can always go back."

Thinking of the miles across the pass, Bannister looked at the gate and the man behind it, and his eyes narrowed. He knew it was common practice in some of the wilder parts of the West — like this back region of Colorado — to throw a fence across a traveled public road and try to collect tolls at the point of a gun. Still, in this case it did appear that some work was being done to maintain the road through rough and hard-wintered country; perhaps it was a legitimate business claim after all.

The gatekeeper spat brownly. "You can argue the rates with Wolford," he suggested, with a jerk of his head toward the log building at his back. "But you'll have to pay, first."

Bannister shrugged, dug up a couple of silver dollars and tossed them over the fence, one by one. They chimed together as the old fellow caught them both out of the air with the same hand, dropped them without a glance into a pocket of his mackinaw. Making no further comment he slipped the loop of wire that held the gate to its post, and swung it wide enough for Bannister to ride through.

Halting again, half turning his mount, Jim Bannister watched as the gate was closed again and fastened. The old fellow moved with shoulders hunched as though the morning chill constricted his muscles.

Bannister asked casually, "Where will this road take me?"

"A little late to be wondering," the other said, cocking a look up at him, "after payin' your two bucks to travel it. Well, it takes you downhill mainly. Colton Creek's there, and the town — same name. It's a good piece. Eighteen, twenty miles as the road lies."

"Cattle country?"

The old man nodded. "A little mining, in the hills — but you don't look much like no hardrock man." He gave a raking scrutiny to the stranger's saddle-whipped length and his gear, and the easy way he sat the leather. "If you're looking for a riding job, now . . ."

"No." Bannister knew at once he had spoken too shortly, as the red-rimmed eyes narrowed and the mouth closed down, drawing the cheek tighter across the bulge of chaw. "I've got no plans, actually," he said in an attempt to undo the damage. "Just more or less riding through."

"I'm sure it's nothin' to me," the man

told him curtly. "I was just goin' to suggest who you might talk to about a job. You can starve, far as I'm concerned."

Bannister could have sworn. He had his own reasons for wanting not to draw attention to himself, but the chance of running into a toll gate, and now an unfortunate remark, had made it certain that this old man would remember the tall rider with the unshorn yellow hair and pale eyes and sharp-edged temper.

Hiding his chagrin, Bannister nodded toward the log building as he asked, in a tone he made pleasant, "Speaking of starving, I wonder if I'd be able to get a meal?"

"I reckon." Grudgingly the man nodded, barely bobbing his head on its long neck, and loosed another gobbet of juice into the mud. His eyes never left their uncomfortable stare on Bannister's face. The latter nodded his thanks, turned the dun and eased on over toward the big, two-storied structure.

As he did, something, the merest flicker of a movement drew his eye to a window on the second floor above the shallow veranda roof. He had no clear look at what was behind the glass; if anyone had been watching his approach, they had already pulled back out of sight. He didn't like this, but having started his intention he could hardly turn aside — not with the gatekeeper's stare following him.

Then the edge of the veranda roof came across, cutting him off from view of that upper row of windows. Deliberately he swung down, tied his reins to a peeled-pole of roof support. A surreptitious movement settled the hang of his holster; Jim Bannister mounted the three slab steps and his bootheels sounded on the porch flooring.

With a tall man's instinct he ducked for clearance as he stepped through the door and inside. Height was his handicap, the identifying mark that thwarted every effort to pass without drawing attention. The most casual stranger was certain to remember him later, when told of a tall, yellow-haired man named Jim Bannister, and of the twelve thousand dollar bounty on his head for the supposed murder of a crooked syndicate agent.

Carrying a price tag like that, the wonder was he still found any place remote enough where he could walk in a door and not be met with the cry, "It's Bannister!" and face a bullet primed to cut him down for the reward.

Here he encountered only silence at first. In the big rock fireplace a burning log snapped and streamed sparks as the flames worked into a pocket of pitch. The room itself was almost bare, with a couple of trestle tables along one wall and a pine plank counter that might have been a bar, facing them. Shelves behind the bar held bottles and glasses and other odds and ends. A board on the wall, with scraps of paper spiked to it, appeared to serve as a general bulletin board. A set of stairs mounted to the second floor, where there were probably sleeping rooms for transients — and where Bannister may or may not have caught someone peering at him from a window.

Through a yonder door, a drifting scent of frying meat reached him. Half starved as he was on saddle rations, that was enough to make his cheek muscles ache as his salivary glands started working.

A man came in from the kitchen. He had a villainous look; he was bald, but with a mustache like a pirate's. He merely stared at the stranger as Bannister said pleasantly, "My nose tells me somebody is doing something to a steak. I wonder if they could be persuaded to do the same to one for me?"

Still without a word or a change of expression, the man signaled with a jerk of the head for him to take a seat at one of the tables. He started to turn away and Bannister added quickly, "Anything you got to go with it, would be welcome. Potatoes, a couple eggs fried solid —"

"It'll take a little time," the man said, the first words he had spoken. He went back into the kitchen. Bannister chose a seat for himself, where he could watch both doors, especially the stairway to the second floor. He laid his hat on the bench beside him.

The wait was a good deal longer than a minute, but at last the man was back with a plate of food and an iron coffee pot, from which he filled one of the china cups ranged along the table. Bannister thanked him, took knife and fork and began to eat. The meat was tough and the eggs and potatoes swam in grease, but he was too hungry to mind. He ate with complete absorption but with an ear attuned for any slight sound that might be heard above the crackling of the burning log. Finished, he drained the last of the bitter coffee, picked up his hat and walked over to the counter, reaching for his money.

His host, Wolford, according to the man on the gate, was puttering around, likely

14

making work while he kept an eye on Bannister to make sure he didn't leave without paying. The price was outrageous but Bannister let it go unchallenged. Putting a gold piece on the counter he asked, "Could I pick up a few supplies? I'm running low."

The other looked at him. "Hell, mister. This ain't no general store. Every can and sack of grub that we use ourselves, has to be hauled up from the railhead."

"All right," Bannister pointed to a shelf behind the man's elbow. "At least I can see a whole box of Bull Durham sacks. I'll have one and papers, please."

Wolford grunted and tossed the makings in front of his guest; after striking the gold piece against the edge of the wood to test its ring, he got out his cashbox. Waiting while he made change, Bannister opened the tobacco sack and rolled a cigarette. He was about to set a match to it when footsteps began to descend the stairs behind him. He turned quickly; above the hands cupped in front of his mouth, he watched the pair who came down.

The woman was a beauty — not tall, but shapely, brown of hair and dark of eyes. The natural grace with which she moved suggested that she could be a good horsewoman, and probably was. She was dressed for traveling, in a becoming brown jacket and skirt, a wrap of some sort over one arm. To Bannister she looked troubled as she turned her head and said something to the man behind her.

He did not answer, or even look at her. His own gaze held narrowly on the face of the stranger at the counter.

Bannister returned the look. He saw a face almost too strong to be handsome, the jaw blunt, the mouth unyielding. The man was well built, broad shouldered, wearing flatcrowned hat and polished boots and a gray suit that appeared expensive. He carried a carpetbag in one hand; Bannister didn't see a gun. He looked about forty, perhaps fifteen years older than the woman.

Her husband?

The interest in the stare that held on Bannister bothered him, and put a cold weight of apprehension in his chest as he got the cigarette drawing. His change was lying in front of him and he scooped up coins and bills and pocketed them. The proprietor was speaking past him now to the couple on the stairs, in a manner that had changed and was now completely deferential. "Good morning! Just have a seat, folks. Your breakfast will be ready for you right away."

The woman thanked him, in a pleasant voice, but the man said nothing at all. As Bannister turned toward the door they were standing at the bottom of the steps and the man's scowling stare, questioning, probing, still rested on the stranger. Deliberately ignoring it, as though unaware of any threat, he turned and walked without haste to the door, and outside.

The gatekeeper had vanished somewhere, about his chores. Bannister went out to his horse, lifted the saddle fender and gave an unneeded tug at the cinch strap. Afterward, he took his time untying, swung easily into the saddle and turned his dun northward, leaving the gate and buildings behind him.

When he glanced back he was distinctly startled to see that the man from the second floor had followed him out and was standing motionless on the veranda's edge, staring after him through the dimly filtered light. His face, and the broad-brimmed white hat, showed only vaguely. But Bannister knew the man was watching him ride away; and he knew now, for certain, who it was that had looked upon him earlier from the window.

It had to mean something. The man's look held more than casual interest; and the chill that touched Bannister's spine, as he rode deliberately away, was due to something other than the low clouds that kept the morning sun hidden.

Coleman Dorsey remained where he was, watching, until the big man on the dun horse was swallowed by the turnings of the wagon road. Afterward he saw the old gatekeeper heading toward the barn, a manure fork on his shoulder, and called him over with a snap of the fingers and a summoning jerk of the head. The man came quickly to halt at the foot of the veranda steps.

"That one that just rode out of here, the big fellow, on the dun. I saw you from upstairs, talking to him when you opened the gate. Somebody you know?"

"Never saw him before," the old man answered.

"What did he want to talk about?"

"Usual thing. He didn't like paying the two bucks. And, he had some questions about the country yonder."

"Questions?" Dorsey picked that up sharply. "Did he mention any names?"

Bristly gray brows puckered. "Not as I remember. Seems like an ordinary sort of drifter to me, Mister Dorsey."

The younger man, his eyes still thoughtful, turned to stare a moment in speculation after the vanished rider; one hand, strong, rope hardened, competent, slapped the leg of his tailored trousers silently. Then with a shrug he swung again toward the door, pausing long enough to fling a final word of instruction; "I'll want my rig hitched and ready to go in twenty minutes." The old man nodded, and Coleman Dorsey went back inside.

Sarah, seated at one of the tables with her wrap lying on the bench at her side, and a coffee cup, untouched, in front of her, looked up quickly as he entered. "Is something wrong?"

Dorsey gave his wife an impatient glance. "Of course not," he said abruptly, and took a place across from her where another mug of black brew stood waiting. "Why should there be?"

"The way you followed that man, in such a hurry. I don't know, I thought perhaps . . ."

"It was nothing," he said with curt indifference, and spooned sugar into his cup. "I had an idea he wanted to speak to me, but apparently not. Whoever he was, he didn't wait."

Stirring the liquid, he looked at her and something in her silent regard made him frown. "You look as though you don't believe me!" he charged. He pointed the bowl of the spoon at her. "You're acting very strangely this morning, do you know that?"

Her brown eyes wavered. For the first time he saw how pale she was beneath her tan. The knuckles of the hands that lay in front of her were white with tension. "I'm sorry!" Sarah Dorsey blurted. "I . . . I really don't know what's come over me. . . . I have the . . . the most awful feeling that something dreadful is happening. I woke up in the night and couldn't go back to sleep." Seeing his expression she shook her head and there was a sudden glint of tears. "Don't be angry with me, Coleman. Please!"

"Angry?" As he said it he was careful to smile and mask the contempt from his voice, the contempt which, after all, was the strongest emotion he felt for any woman, even this beautiful creature across the table who was his wife. "Now, that's foolishness," he told her, indulgently. "And so are these female hunches of yours. You must pay them no mind."

Shaking her head, she lifted a hand and let it drop again. "I *try* not to. This morning, I just can't help it."

When he reached across and covered her hand with his, he found it cold under his fingers. "You're tired," he assured her. "It's been a hard trip, and I don't think anybody could sleep much in that bed! Now, eat up," he finished bruskly, as Bill Wolford came in from the kitchen bringing plates of food. "We can be home by noon. And no more of these premonitions, you hear?"

He smiled and squeezed her hand. But the eyes that watched her turn to her plate were speculative and cold.

Chapter 2

Resting his horse, Jim Bannister looked at the land that had opened ahead of him with rather startling abruptness. He could see the flash of a waterfall that was probably the beginning of the Colton Creek, and widening glimpses of a valley hemmed by shouldering ranges. The road dropped from here, swiftly, to fall away presently in a series of switchbacks down a nearly vertical drop of sheer granite.

So he knew the reason for the steep charge at the toll gate: this was a made road; it had taken money and effort to tear it out of the rock and open a way for wheel travel across the passes, and it would be an expensive job keeping it in repair. Bannister eyed those steep switchbacks, thinking that a man caught out in the open would be an easy and helpless target for an enemy with a rifle, like shooting a fly off a windowpane. The longer he looked, remembering the cold eyes of the stranger at the toll house, the less this appealed to him.

He at least wanted to check out his back trail before he tried it. Just above the point where he was sitting, a washout had spilled gravel and loose rock from a gully mouth and offered a way for the dun to climb out of the trail without leaving clear sign. On an impulse he sent the dun that way. The horse slipped and scrambled briefly, and then it gained the shelter of the gully; Bannister drew up at a point where screening brush let him study the way he had just come.

Nothing stirred there, though he waited out a slow half hour. He finally had to admit that he just might have been unduly worried about the man who stared at him from the window and later followed him outside. But he still could not feel easy about it. . . .

But now Bannister had made a discovery. Once, it appeared, there had been another trail. Only a horse track, and now badly overgrown and all but obliterated, it was still visible where it snaked its way through the timber to spill into the head of this gully. At one time, he reasoned, this must have been the pass trail before it was replaced by a dug road usable by wheeled traffic. From the look of it, it was now no longer used and perhaps even forgotten.

A trail other men had forgotten looked good to Jim Bannister, just then, if it went where he wanted to go and kept him away from curious eyes, like those of the man at the toll station. It could be a stroke of luck that he had stumbled onto this one.

He spoke to the dun, and swung his bridles toward the gully's head.

Ankle-deep now in hillside rubble, Bannister stood close against a stunted pine and, with one hand resting on his holstered gun, narrowly studied a clump of brush a half dozen yards below him.

The dun, behind him in the trees, stomped impatiently but he neither moved nor took his eyes off that particular spot that had him puzzled. Something was there, something of a tawny yellow color and of no shape he could identify. Alert as he was for anything suspicious, it had brought him down from the saddle while he took a careful look. The poor light, filtered through thickening clouds, dulled colors and hampered his vision. Baffled, he stood motionless as he tried to puzzle this out.

And then the thing before him shifted position, barely, but enough to identify it as a horse standing almost hidden by the scrub. He saw muscle flow beneath a haunch, and the slight flick of the tail. Instantly he dropped to a crouch, his gun in hand.

A horse meant there could be a man, perhaps even now closing in on him. He turned for a look at the dun, wondering if something might have disturbed it a moment ago. But nothing moved except for a damp-smelling breeze that stirred the rank growth crowding about him, bringing a promise of rain.

There was only a horse, standing motionless, where he wouldn't have expected one to be.

Slowly he straightened, and juggled the weight of the gun in his palm while he considered. He could not afford to overlook this; and so, moving carefully, alert for danger, he left his place and walked forward over the treacherous, shifting footing, the weapon ready. Cautiously he eased through the bushes without disturbing them and came beside the horse, a solid, deep-chested claybank gelding. He saw it carried a brand, a Hatchet. It stood under saddle, and as it brought its head around to look at him he saw that trailing reins had tangled in the brush and this, apparently had anchored it. From the droppings it must have been standing there for hours.

Bannister placed a hand on the animal's rump as he holstered the gun. The saddle was a good, serviceable rig, free of embossing or other ornament. Suddenly he looked more closely, and touched the leather with a finger, and felt a revulsion at the sticky thickness of blood that had nearly, but not quite, dried.

He stared at his hand, seeing the evidence of a tragedy. Someone had been shot, it must have been several hours ago. Still, whatever the fate of the claybank's rider, it plainly had nothing to do with him, Bannister concluded as he wiped his fingers on his pantleg. He reached for the animal's reins then, thinking to jerk them free and hook them over the saddlehorn and start the animal off; it would return to its home corral. But in that moment his eye discovered another splotch of blood, this one smeared across the surface of a rock. He could see now where the brush was broken and flattened, as though someone had fallen headlong.

Quickly Bannister lifted his head. Directly in front of him, and up a slight grade from where he stood, angled a line of weathered caprock. The lower portions had collapsed and fallen away, leaving a hollow that was darkly shadowed in this cloud-dimmed light. It looked like a place where a wounded animal, or man, might go to earth. Jim Bannister left the claybank where it was and began to climb.

The body lay face down in a limp sprawl, just under the shelter of the overhang. The back of his jacket was soaked with clotted blood. At first glance he looked as dead as he would ever be, and with genuine distaste Bannister went down on one knee to turn him over. No one he had even seen before, of course — a man perhaps in his fifties, though with a face so worked upon by all kinds of weather it would be hard to judge. His thick shock of hair held a generous sprinkling of silver.

Bannister looked at him, helplessly scowling; but in the next moment it occurred to him there might be a faint lifting of the man's chest. He felt for a heartbeat, was not sure. Hastily then he tore open the front of the man's coat and placed an ear against him, and made out the definite slow rhythm of his breathing.

There was a scrape of cloth, the click of a gun-sear. Startled he drew back, staring into pain-drugged eyes and into the gaping bore of a revolver.

His mouth went quickly dry. The hurt

man might be out of his head and unable even to hold the wavering gunmuzzle steady; even so, at that point blank range he could hardly miss blowing a hole through Bannister the size of a tunnel. Now the bloodless lips moved, a tortured whisper stirred them: "I've got *one* of you, anyway!"

Moving without hurry, Bannister closed a palm over the gun's barrel and hammer spur, to prevent the mechanism working. He felt a feeble pull of the trigger, saw beads of sweat spring out on that other, ashen face. Then the hurt man's arm began to shake violently and Bannister lifted the gun from his fingers and laid it aside.

"Get ahold of yourself," he said gently. "I'm not part of them, whoever it was did this to you. I want to help you if you'll let me. But first, we've got to see just how bad you're hurt."

He couldn't tell if his words got through. His strength drained by the thwarted effort with the gun, the other looked to have slipped again into unconsciousness. Bannister could get no response from him; he proceeded anyway to the distasteful chore of examining the damage.

It didn't look good, the bullet had entered at the back and was still inside. Bannister would be willing to guess the man had lain in this hole overnight. His wound did not seem to be bleeding now, but that was not assurance he wasn't bleeding internally. Again, the bullet might only be lodged in the thick muscles of his back, or resting against a bone. The only thing Bannister knew for certain, with no better tool than a clasp knife, was he didn't dare try probing for it. Nor was it safe to think of moving him.

At a loss, he settled back to stare at the unconscious man. There wasn't much to know about him. A quick search of his clothing had produced no further identification, beyond the Hatchet brand on his claybank.

Reminded of the animal, Bannister went out and got it and his own dun horse and moved them nearer to the cave, into a grassy hollow where there was a clear seep spring, the dun could use the feed and rest, while he tended the hurt man. The claybank, after its long hours in the brush, was thirsty enough and hungry too; Bannister slipped the bit so it could graze, and eased the saddle. Afterward he got materials from his own pack, dipped up a panful of spring water, and went back into the cave.

What was needed, plainly, was a doctor. There seemed to be no particular fever, not as yet anyhow. But the longer that wound went without adequate care, the worse the odds. Bannister did what he could, and afterward ducked outside and stood scowling at the tumble of hills and rock and timber that fell away from this high point.

This was surely the last thing in the world anyone in his position could afford to get involved with — anyone with a price on his head and a hangrope waiting — unless he could somehow prove the murder he was condemned for had been no murder. If the thing had been reversed, did he really suppose that this stranger, or any other, would have risked his neck to take responsibility for him? But, reasoning of that sort didn't do much good. The fact remained that a man lay helpless, and desperately wounded; and only Jim Bannister was here to help.

Suddenly he stiffened. The clouds had been thickening and the day was darker than ever, with a cold wind come up now to lash the brush and treeheads beneath a black sky. Yet despite the poor visibility, he had glimpsed some kind of movement below him.

There were glasses in a case on his saddle; quickly he went and got them, and adjusting the lenses, searched and picked it up again: a group of horsemen threading across an open break in the timber. He counted four; then they were in the trees again, but not before he satisfied himself that they were coming directly toward him. He watched a moment longer. Then, with a growing sense of urgency, he turned and went back into the cave and knelt to put a hand on the hurt man's shoulder.

"Can you hear me?" he demanded.

No response; the other could have been dead except for the continued faint breathing. But now the eyes wavered open, and after a moment Bannister saw them come to focus. He spoke again, slowly and distinctly, as though he were talking to a deaf person. "There's four riders headed this way. I think they're following your sign."

He let this sink in, saw it take effect. Understanding showed, and then alarm and fear flooded in and displaced the dullness in the unwinking stare. Quickly, Bannister said, "I was just wondering, could these be friends trying to find you?"

The pallid lips moved. "Friends!" the man repeated, in a voice like a croak. "I learned yesterday I got no friends. If they find me they'll kill me."

Such abject despair had its effect. Bannister's hand found the other's shoulder, closed on it reassuringly. "Take it easy," he said. "Nothing's going to happen."

The pain-filled stare searched his face. "I don't know you. But whoever you are — mix in it and they'll kill you too!"

"I don't plan to let them." Bannister knew now what had to be done. He said, "I'm going to take the claybank. I have an idea I can lead them away from you. Here's your gun," he added, placing it under the limp hand. "And I've brought water."

"Water."

He took the pan he'd filled at the spring, and raising the man as carefully as he could put it to his lips. Much spilled down his chin but he managed a couple of swallows. He groaned as he was eased back again, and his eyes closed.

"There's jerky, too," Bannister said. "If you can manage it." There was no answer; perhaps the man had lost consciousness. He couldn't stay to find out. Bannister ducked out from under the low rock overhang, and a moment later was heading at a run for the place where he left the horses.

Chapter 3

Working under pressure, he got the saddle off the dun but then merely dumped it into the bushes, there was not time to make a switch to the claybank, or even adjust the stirrups on the saddle it already bore, even though he knew they would be much too short. The animal was reluctant, after standing so many hours under saddle, but Bannister quickly mounted up and headed him downslope, as though intending to meet those other riders making their way up toward him through the trees.

He knew his strategy. The glasses had shown where the timber was broken by barren rock, slippage from some old fault line. He saw only one narrow break the hunted man could have used in getting past, and his sign was leading the searchers straight toward that. So it seemed the logical place to start laying false trail.

The claybank, luckily, had left little sign in the sliderock and pine litter; an expert tracker could probably have picked it up, but he didn't mean for anyone to take that close a look. Doubling back he reached the break in the rock reef, pulled in briefly to listen. Then, swinging the horse about, Bannister started off in a new direction that angled sharply away from that cave, up under the rimrock where the hurt man lay.

Almost at once he found the animal's hoofs sinking deep as they gouged into loose rock and gravel. When he glanced back, he saw the trail he was leaving and gave a grunt of satisfaction.

No chance of those tracks being missed! Now if he could only be sure none of the searchers had eyes sharp enough to notice that the sign they followed had suddenly grown fresh.

He reached timber and its welcome protection closed about him; his impulse was to keep riding and put distance behind him, but he made himself pull up and, turning in the saddle, leaned to peer beneath the branches. Almost immediately he saw a horseman appear in the break and halt there as a second one joined him, and then two more. They conferred briefly, pointing at the ground as they talked. Then they were coming ahead, following the sign Bannister had left for them; four riders, strung out in single file, and close enough now for him to see even without the glasses the belt guns they wore, and the rifles that stood in more than one saddle holster.

It looked as though they had done what he wanted, but in tolling them away from their intended victim he had put them on his own trail, and uncomfortably near. Bannister lifted the reins and kicked the claybank, and went on through the ranks of the trees searching for the best route.

He felt an occasional cold lance of rain sting his face; the sound of the horse's hooves was sopped up by the litter of fallen needles. Presently they climbed to the comb of a secondary ridge, and followed this for some distance before dropping into the ravine beyond, where the trees thinned above the course of a boulder-clogged stream. The horse was reluctant to enter this but Bannister forced him, anxious now to drown the trail he'd taken such pains to lay. He walked his horse down though the shallow, swift water that churned and boiled and gave the claybank trouble keeping on its feet.

Just above a drop-off point where the stream fell away in a lacy cataract, he found a place to climb out. The farther bank was steep and the claybank's steel struck sparks from naked rock as it slipped and fought for purchase. When they got up into the trees again, the animal was breathing hard and Bannister let it rest, taking this moment to dismount and, belatedly, let out the stirrups to a length that suited him.

Afterwards, on again, the rain was coming harder now. He fell into a deer trail that promised better time. With spruce and lodgepole pine crowding him, he could almost begin to believe he'd lost the pursuers, but even so he still faced the question of what he was going to do about the wounded man in that hole under the rimrock.

Suddenly the timber thinned and a tilted bench opened up, strewn with bolders and crisscrossed with the trails of driven cattle. Above him would be the summer range for stock ranches of the Colton Creek district; crews might already be moving their herds up, as the last of winter lifted from the high country and the mountain meadows dried out. Bannister would as soon not run into any other horsemen, and actually he caught no sign of any. Once, as he pushed through a wet stand of brush, he startled a deer and sent it bounding off, and his fingers groped for gunmetal before his taut nerves settled again.

Then, breaking past a shoulder of rock into what had looked like another shallow ravine, he saw he had made a mistake. For, almost at once, the walls fell back and grew steeper, and presently a sheer rock face, green with lichens, rose before him. He had ridden into a natural cove, seemingly with no other exit. Not wanting to believe that he was trapped, he rode on, searching out the brush and the few scant trees, looking for a break in the walls that the claybank could negotiate. But there was neither a way out, nor a good place to hide. Bannister swore, and, pulling the horse around, rode hurriedly back the way he had come.

As he cleared the opening he heard, faintly, a shout.

He reined violently to the right, kicked with the spurs. As the claybank lunged ahead, there was a flat crack of a rifle; the sound was taken up and multiplied in rolling echoes by the mist-shrouded peaks. The bullet came nowhere near but it told him his efforts had been in vain, he hadn't shaken pursuit, and the time just lost could prove fatal.

In front of him a fan of talus from some old slide, high as a house and crowned with a tangle of uprooted trees, blocked the way. With more time he could have worked past it, but looking at it now he saw there was no chance. A glance back showed him the horsemen, drawing nearer and spreading out to head him off if he tried to double past.

Six-shooters and rifles in their hands gleamed dully through the thickening spears of rain. Deliberately, Bannister reined the claybank around to face them. He laid both hands on the saddlehorn, in plain sight, and with a deliberately expressionless face he watched them close in.

In a group like this you could generally single out the leader, and Bannister did so. He was not a big man, but he looked solid and with a certain hard competence about him. Heavy, beetling brows struck harshly above a broad-cheeked face that had been weathered out to the color and texture of saddle leather. He came a little ahead of the others, at last drawing rein a couple of yards distance to scan the stranger's face with hard black eyes.

"Anybody know him?" he demanded of his followers, and got only headshakes. "All right!" he told Bannister. "Whoever you are, we'll quit playing games. Where is he?"

It was raining harder. All four of the

riders had, at some point, found time to don slickers that shone wetly in the dull light, but Bannister's was still strapped behind his saddle, back where he'd left the dun. He was actually aware of the chill damp soaking into his clothing. He returned the leader's stare as he said, "I haven't any idea who you're talking about."

The dark face took on an impatient scowl. "Oh, come on! The man you got the horse from. Where did you leave him?"

"There wasn't any man," Bannister lied. "I saw the animal running loose. I was afoot and figured I had as much need of him as anyone. I helped myself."

"Don't give me that!" The words shot at him, ugly and dangerous. "And don't think we can't get the truth out of you!" A carbine lay across the man's broad thighs, a stubby finger through the trigger guard. The weapon lifted and the black ring of its muzzle pointed at the stranger's chest.

Bannister looked at it, trying to keep his face expressionless. One of the other riders, a redfaced man with the rusty horns of a lank mustache framing his mouth, rubbed a fist over it and said uneasily, "Quint, you suppose he's telling the truth? Maybe he did find him. Wouldn't be the first range bum that thought he seen a chance to make away with a good piece of horseflesh."

Quint snapped at him, without taking his eyes from the prisoner. "Ain't how I read the sign. I think the two of them met and traded off."

"Then how come we never seen any other tracks?"

"That's just what I aim to find out! His gun, Tacker."

Still looking dubious, the redhead kneed his mount forward keeping out of line of that carbine and, easing up beside the prisoner, slipped the six-shooter out of his holster. Bannister wasn't foolish enough to protest. But in an injured tone he exclaimed, "It would be nice if I had some idea what this is all about."

"Guess!" Quint challenged.

Bannister stared about at the grim faces. Now that Tacker had moved, he had a look for the first time at the brand on the shoulder of the redhead's mount; It was a Hatchet, identical to the one the claybank carried. Frowning he quickly searched the other animals, saw the same brand on all of them. A cold knot of doubt began to form inside him.

"It begins to look," he said bitterly, "as

though I'm riding a stolen horse!"

It had simply never occurred to him that the wounded man in the cave, the man for whom he'd assumed such risks, might not be anything more than a common horse thief! The appalling thought must have shown in his face, for Quint's broad mouth suddenly stretched into a knowing smirk. The man nodded. "So maybe now," he suggested heavily, "you'll make things easier on yourself, and tell us what's become of him that you got it from."

Still, Bannister hesitated. He knew he was being given a way out, but something here didn't quite ring true. He couldn't bring himself to deliver the wounded man into the hands of his enemies, not while so many questions remained unanswered.

He shook his head. "I told you before. I didn't get the horse from anybody. I found him."

There was a kind of stillness. Restless mounts stomped and the rain blew in the wind, and Quint and Tacker and the others continued to stare at Bannister as though waiting for something further. Then Quint's eyes narrowed and he swore, very softly, between his teeth. He straightened thick shoulders and turned his head to look long at a big pine tree and Bannister saw the thought building.

Quite deliberately Quint took down the grass rope that hung in a coil on his saddle. He ran it through his hands and said, "Have it your way. One horse thief will serve as well as another." And to Tacker, with a nod: "Fetch him over here."

His riders needed no instructions. The reins of the claybank were snatched from Bannister's hands; his arms were seized, his hands pulled behind him and tied with a swift efficiency. And now Jim Bannister found himself moved into position beneath a jutting limb of the pine with rain whispering in the needles above his head. Quint had a noose fashioned; he stood in the stirrups and flipped the rope end up over the limb, caught and snubbed it with a quick turn or two about his saddlehorn. The noose swung before the prisoner's eyes.

He tried in vain not to stare at it, knowing his face must show the sick horror inside him. This was the nightmare he had been living with for many months. And suddenly it had come true.

Quint was watching him closely, with a kind of cold ferocity. "Time's running short for you," he told Bannister. "You sure you haven't thought of something you want to say to us?" When he got no answer his mouth hardened; with no further preliminary he deftly slipped the noose over the prisoner's head. The knot tightened. At the feel of the rope, the prisoner's flesh crawled and a cold dribble of sweat broke and ran along his ribs.

A touch of Quint's heels sent his big roan horse backing a bare step. It was movement enough to take up the slack in the rope, and a little more; pulled straight up, his head canted awkwardly by the thick knot against his ear, Bannister could feel the blood beating heavily in his throat and the first hard constriction shutting off his wind. But his stare held steadily on the dark face in front of him, even as blackness began to swim across his eyes and his head filled with a dull roaring.

Someone a great distance away was shouting. "You want to talk now?" His lips managed to say no though he knew no sound came out.

How long the moment lasted, Bannister could never judge; it seemed an age. Then the pull on the rope was eased so abruptly he had to brace himself to avoid sliding from the saddle. He was still unable to breathe, but an instant later someone jerked roughly at the noose, loosening it, and it was flipped over his head. Welcome air, chill and pungent, flooded his lungs.

Chapter 4

As his vision cleared, Bannister saw the man named Quint coiling the rope and scowling. "You got nerve!" Quint said grudgingly. "I have to give you that much. But don't get the idea it's gonna gain you anything. Sooner or later you'll tell me what I want to know."

Bannister only looked at him. "And while he's stalling," one of the others said sourly, "Hardman's getting clean away from us."

Hardman! So now the wounded man had a name.

"I doubt he's getting far," declared the one called Tacker. "I hit him, I tell you. I hit him bad. I always know when I miss a shot, and I didn't miss that one! If we ain't found him, it's because he's gone to earth someplace, and this saddle bum knows where!"

"Maybe he knows, but he sure ain't telling!"

Suddenly the redhead lost his temper. "By God, he will!" He rammed his horse at

45

Bannister's and, grabbing a handful of the prisoner's clothing, hauled him around for a look into the bore of a sixgun. "Speak up! You know what happens if you try holding out on us!"

When there was no answer, the cruel mouth twisted between its drooping horns of rusty mustache; the barrel of the gun made a chopping sideward slash. Bannister tried to move away from it, but the front sight clipped him behind the ear, knocking off his hat and making his whole head ring like a bell.

He would have slid from the saddle but Quint swore and grabbed him roughly, holding him in place. The big man shouted, "Enough of that! He's got something now to chew on; we'll let him work on it while we backtrack. If he don't decide to talk before we find for ourselves where we got thrown off — *then* we'll hang him!" The cold words held a promise and a threat.

Scowling, Tacker said, "What if this damn rain has the sign washed out?"

"It ain't raining that hard yet."

There was no more argument. Quint slashed the rope that bound the prisoner's wrists, less out of consideration, he thought, than to keep from being slowed by a rider trying to keep his balance with both hands tied behind him. Surrounded, and with the claybank's reins anchored to Tacker's saddlehorn, there was no great danger of him getting away.

Grimly Jim Bannister looked at his predicament. He had no illusions. Even if he had been ready to take these men to the one they were hunting, he knew that wouldn't be the end of it, for he was now convinced this was no simple case of horse stealing. Whoever Hardman was, they wanted him to kill him, and what did some nameless range tramp matter? The hurt man had spoken the simple truth: "They'll kill you too if you mix in it!"

Bannister swallowed painfully within his ropesore throat, and wondered how soon impatience would set them to working him over again.

They rode in silence, except as now and then a man would swear when his mount slipped in greasy mud, or when the runnel of rainwater from the brim of a tilted hat spilled down the collar of his slicker. The prisoner, the only one without hat or raincoat, was now soaked through and thoroughly chilled. Numbly he watched the landmarks of his flight slide by in reverse order, with a growing tension now as he saw they were approaching the rock reef where he had first tried to throw them off Hardman's track.

His stare fastened itself on the figure of Quint in the lead, apprehensively watching his shoulders and the back of his head for the first sign that Quint's sharp eyes had noticed something he missed before. Thus it was that he saw Quint pull rein suddenly to stare at the ground, then raise his head for a long look, upslope, at the dark rock and timber where shrouds of mist drifted.

As the breath clogged in Bannister's throat, Tacker called forward sharply, "What is it? You see something?"

No answer, for a moment. Then, whatever thought might have been stirring in him, Quint shrugged it away and turned his horse down into the break in the rock. The others followed, single file. And Jim Bannister breathed again.

Nothing was solved. But now, at least every step would carry them farther from Hardman's place of hiding.

The rate of descent was much quicker, with the rain-shrouded peaks at their backs. The steady course Hardman had followed, until at last the bullet he carried dumped him out of the saddle, showed that he was no stranger to this country but a man who knew where he'd been going. Losing altitude, the cavalcade entered a region of timber and benches of grass that looked, to Bannister, like good summer graze just waiting for cattle to be moved up onto them. The rain had slacked off but now it came harder again. A wind rose, to lash at bent heads and hunched shoulders.

They halted abruptly as one of the men quickly pulled rein, confronting his chief. "We're being made fools of!" he said loudly, in a dark and savage temper. "We should have found Hardman by this time. Me and the boys chased him almost this far last night, before we lost him. So where the hell is he? We're wasting time, and wearing out our horses for nothing."

Quint stared at him coldly, and then turned his attention to the prisoner, while the tired horses stomped and blew streamers of steam into the chill. "Maybe," Quint suggested, "you better get ready to talk."

"I'll get him ready!"

It was the gaunt one, with the rusty drooping mustache, who Bannister had heard called by the name of Sid Tacker. He came shoving his way among the other horsemen, Bannister, twisting about, saw his angry face and had a glimpse of the

49

loop in a saddle rope as it reached for him. Before he could duck away, the noose dropped and settled and his arms were trapped. And when Tacker hit with the spur his horse gave a lunge. The rope bit deep. Helpless, Bannister felt himself lifted bodily from the saddle.

He managed somehow to land on his feet, even to run a few stumbling steps before being jerked and thrown headlong. With both arms pinned, he had no way at all to protect his face as he went spinning at rope's end behind Tacker's mount.

Slop and mud choked him, spiny brush tore at his skin and clothing. At a gallop now, the animal changed directions and the rope sang tautly, whipping him about like a fish played on a line. Dimly, through the confusion of his senses and the bruising punishment, he could hear the Hatchet riders shouting. Suddenly they were all about him, their horses' hoofs shaking the ground so that, any moment, he expected to be swept under. A single swipe from one of those iron shoes would batter the brains out of his skull.

Then, everything stopped.

Bannister, dazed, heard Tacker's horse blowing and the man's harsh challenge: "You want more? Or are you ready yet to — ?" The words broke off. There were other, puzzling sounds, and a growing tremor he could feel through the ground under him. The prisoner managed to lift his face out of the muck, craning his whole upper body for a bewildered look.

He had an impression of a shifting wall of red hides darkened by the rain, of dully glinting horns, of a shuttling confusion of legs and hooves plodding toward him at eye level in a mist of kicked up, muddy water. In that moment it seemed to Bannister the cattle were heading directly for him, and it was instinct that made him stir, fighting his own numbness and the rope that held him tight. Somehow he got up onto his knees, and then staggered drunkenly to his feet and stumbled backward until the shoulder of Tacker's horse stopped him; there he stood swaying on his boots, watching the animals that had spilled out of the rocks below this brushy meadow and were slogging past toward a screen of timber at its head.

He saw now that a pair of horsemen had detached themselves from the herd and were pulled up at a little distance, staring at the Hatchet riders, and at the prisoner anchored by rope to Sid Tacker's saddlehorn. It was one of these newcomers who blurted, in a startled voice, "What the devil's going on?"

"None of your business!" Russ Quint snapped.

But Tacker, showing his teeth in a grin, said at almost the same moment, "What does it look like, Ingram? We're getting set to hang us a horse thief!"

The newcomers exchanged a look. Ingram, the one who had spoken, seemed reluctant to interfere still further. Still, he frowned and said, "Ain't that kind of drastic? We got laws to take care of such things."

"You can go to the devil!" the redhead answered and backed his horse a step, with a savage jerk at the line that staggered Bannister and dropped him sprawling. This cruelty appeared to be more than Ingram could take. He swore and lifted his hand from his lap, revealing that it held a gun with the muzzle pointed at Tacker.

"I think you better let him go."

"Like hell!"

But the sight of the weapon seemed to have caught all the Hatchet riders by surprise. Sid Tacker scowled at it, and at Ingram; then, with a sour grimace, he gave the rope a flip that freed it from its dally about the horn. He flung the loose end into the mud.

"Keep an eye on them, Mort," the one called Ingram told his companion, and kneed his horse forward to where the prisoner had regained his feet. His expression was sober as he leaned, worked loose the loop and slipped it over Bannister's head and tossed it aside.

Quint, the leader of the Hatchet men, spoke in heavy warning. "You're making a mistake! This man's nothing but a range tramp. We caught him with a stolen horse and we figure to give him what he has coming."

Ingram would be in his early thirties Bannister judged, wiry of build, with a sparse beard and untrimmed hair of the same color. He demanded of the prisoner, "What do *you* say?"

Still shaken from the experience of being dragged, Jim Bannister put up a hand and pulled it across scratched and muddy cheeks. He shook his head, repeating the story he had made up for the Hatchet men. It was lame enough, but the best he could do without telling the truth and involving the wounded Hardman. "I never stole anything," he said gruffly. "I was afoot and I needed a horse, and I saw the claybank. I would have turned him loose again when I could."

"Is that the animal?" Ingram peered at the riderless horse. His eyes narrowed. "Man! You pick good when you're doing it!"

His companion was an older man, with sharp eyes and a pointed, aggressive jaw; the brown horse he rode bore the same 3W brand as the cattle. He had pulled a carbine from his saddle holster and was holding it gingerly in both hands. He said, with a look at Bannister, "No wonder you're in trouble! You went and grabbed old man Hardman's own saddler!"

The prisoner stared back, made speechless by what he had just heard. It was *not* a stolen horse then, and never had been. And Hardman, too, must be a Hatchet, the same as Quint, and Tacker, and these others who were bent on finding and killing him! Bannister had been puzzled before; now he was bewildered.

The last struggle of beef had passed by now, to vanish in a dark belt of pine at the head of the clearing. A couple of punchers who had been pushing them, mounted on 3W-branded horses, dropped back and rode over. They saw the situation and, rather uncertainly, it appeared to Bannister, drew their belt guns. To the prisoner, standing helpless on the ground between the two groups, they appeared to be matched fairly evenly. A dangerous tension spun out into the diminishing sound of cattle moving away.

It was Russ Quint who announced darkly, "I'll say it just once. You still got a chance to put up those guns and ride away from here, and leave us to finish this."

Ingram retorted flatly, "Sorry, but I ain't going to let a man be hanged just to please Hatchet."

Quint looked at the one with the carbine. "And you, Mort Woods? What have you got to say?"

Before Woods could give him an answer, a new voice called up from the cluster of rocks where the cattle had first come into sight. Turning his head, Bannister thought he could make out the head and upper body of someone with the barrel of a long gun resting across the top of a boulder. "Hey!" he shouted. He sounded young, his voice high-pitched with excitement. "Farley, I got my sights lined up on Russ Quint's right ear. A shot like this, I couldn't miss!"

"All right, kid," Farley Ingram called back quickly. "Just don't get excited. That rifle of yours has an awful easy trigger pull."

If that was intended for a warning to Quint, it had its effect. The Hatchet man had started to jerk his head about, but he thought better of it and froze; his dark face visibly lost color. And Bannister, seeing how this had tipped the balance, felt it was time for him to make some appeal to reason. "There's no good sense," he began, "letting this come to a shooting. . . ."

They ignored him. Ingram, alone, gave him the barest glance and a shake of the head. "It ain't over you," he said gruffly. "In fact, you got damn little to do with it; this has been building. Best thing for you to do, is take the claybank and get out of here."

"Don't touch that horse!" Russ Quint bawled. But with a rifle trained at his head he made no actual move.

Jim Bannister had a decision to make. It was becoming clear that, whatever lay behind this confrontation, he no less than the claybank was simply a pawn in it. That being the case, nothing he did or said was likely to make much difference; and meanwhile he had himself to think about. And not only himself. At the moment he was still the only hope for the wounded Nat Hardman.

So, moving carefully, he got the claybank's reins and, having led him into the clear where he would not place himself between the two groups of men, toed the stirrup and swung astride. He hesitated. He wanted to ask for the return of his gun, in Sid Tacker's saddle pocket, but knew that would be pressing too hard. He started to tell Farley Ingram, "I'd just like to say I'm grateful —"

The man shook his head without taking eyes off Russ Quint. "No time for that," he cut in. "You best get out of here."

"I got something to add," Ingram's hardeyed companion said sharply. "Could be you're no more than a harmless saddle tramp, but just the same I'll give you a little warning of my own. Let me catch you around any of my 3W horses, and I just might hang you myself. Now, beat it!"

Bannister felt the tightening of the muscles in his jaw. Stung pride brought an angry reply rushing to his tongue but he bit it back. He knew how he must appear, just then — rainsoaked, muddy and bedraggled, shivering in another man's saddle with one cheek smeared with blood where it had been scraped raw at the end of Sid Tacker's lass rope.

He turned the claybank and rode away,

across hoof-torn earth where the cattle had passed. But at the last moment, still disturbed by the violence in the two groups of riders he had left sitting like statues in their rain-wet slickers, he drew rein for a moment at the edge of the timber and glanced back.

Mort Woods must have been keeping him in the tail of his eye. Now, seeing him halt, the 3W owner twisted about, and the carbine snapped up to his shoulder and loosed a shot in Bannister's direction. The voice of the weapon flatted off alarmingly in the drizzle; the bullet thunked into the wet ground close enough to make the claybank snort and start to rear. Mort Woods shouted, "You *git!*"

Bannister, shaken, had no choice. He shrugged and wrenched the animal's head around. The trees quickly swallowed him, and the scene in the clearing was left behind.

Chapter 5

For a moment Farley Ingram thought that the lash of Mort Woods's rifle, so completely unexpected, would break a tense situation completely apart. His own nervous reaction, transmitted through a tight rein, caused the animal under him to toss its head and move around under him a little; as he tried to settle it, he saw Russ Quint break his pose and begin a downward motion of one arm toward the gun in his belt holster.

His own hands full settling the horse, Ingram had no hope of stopping him. But Woods was quicker than might have been expected. Even as the stranger on the claybank disappeared into the trees, he was whipping about again, levering a fresh cartridge. And Russ Quint, just in time, checked his arm movement and instead brought the hand up and placed it on the saddlehorn.

Ingram saw him turn to check on that other rifle in the rocks below them. When he turned back Quint's scowl was dark;

his cheeks, wet with rain, gleamed faintly. His stare rested on Farley Ingram as he demanded loudly, "Have you had enough of this foolishness? I thought you, of all people, had more sense than to pick a fight with Hatchet — and for no better cause than some nameless range tramp."

"If our differences with Hatchet have to come to a fight," Ingram replied, in a tone that he was sure must sound as heavy as his spirits at that moment, "then I guess it will come. It don't matter over what."

"I can promise you, it will come damn quick if you don't stand clear and let us get after that bastard!"

But, reluctant as he might be to welcome trouble, when well in it this Farley Ingram had a stubborn streak and it was stiffening now. Unyielding, he shook his head at the Hatchet range boss and answered, "I'll have no part of a lynching and that's what you're after."

Quint swiveled his angry stare to the 3W owner. "And you, Woods? It means nothing at all to you that the man's a horse thief?"

The latter shrugged inside his stiff rubber slicker. "If he had to steal something, better old man Hardman's nag than one of mine. Far from concerned, I make him a present of the claybank. Then maybe he'll leave my own stuff be!" He added, the rifle muzzle describing a small circle as he gestured with it, "Maybe the four of you better get rid of that hardware. Shuck the guns and belts and throw them on the ground."

Russ Quint seemed to swell in size. Beside him, Sid Tacker leaned and shouted furiously, "By God, no! The only part of my gun that you'll take is a slug in your belly!" As he spoke he deliberately pushed aside the skirt of his raincoat and, defying the guns in the nervous hands of the riders he faced, laid a red-furred hand upon the butt of his holstered gun.

Something like an iron fist clenched inside Farley Ingram, stopping his breath, for he was certain everything was about to blow apart. But the tableau held, the moment froze at the edge of violence. Then Russ Quint said gruffly, "The hell with this!" He barked an order; at the same time, a drag at the reins backed and turned his roan and the three Hatchet riders with him broke their grouping. Even Tacker, with a last black glare for those who had faced Hatchet down, wrenched his animal's head around. Spurs kicked home.

It was not a rout. Hatchet had failed to

get past a determined resistance, but neither had they given up their guns; there was a cold deliberateness about the way they showed their backs, and they rode without haste. When they passed from sight beyond a bay of rock and scrub, Ingram heard Mort Woods let out his breath raggedly. There was a creaking of wet leather as one of Woods's punchers finally remembered to ease his cramped position in the saddle.

No one had so much as moved, for a longer period than they had realized.

Farley Ingram felt his own hand shaking a little as he raised it and put two fingers to his lips and loosed a shrill whistle toward the rock where his brother Bob was forted up. He circled a fist beside his hatbrim, saw Bob's rifle barrel swing once above his head in answer to the signal. Moments later the kid himself came into view, mounted on his sorrel, still carrying his rifle by the balance as he came spurring to join them.

He fairly danced in the stirrups; his high-boned cheeks, with their few straggling dark hairs that didn't yet need regular shaving, were pale with excitement. "I guess we showed Hatchet that time!" he exclaimed before he even brought the sorrel to a halt. "I was pushing up the stragglers when I seen you squaring off, and I figured the thing for me to do was stay back and put 'em between us. Wish I could of seen Quint's face when he knew I had my rifle on him!"

Bob's impulsiveness was always a concern to his more conservative elder brother, who suspected the difference between them was even more a matter of temperament than it was the nearly ten years' difference in their ages. Now, frowning, he had to agree: "You done fine, boy. You made 'em think a couple of times."

"But, *you!*" his brother exclaimed admiringly. "Without I watched you standing off Russ Quint and Sid Tacker and making 'em back down, I never would of believed it! What was it all about, anyhow? Who was the feller that rode away on old Hardman's claybank?"

Mort Woods answered him. "He was nothing at all, some drifter or other, a horse thief at that. But Tacker was dragging him, and there was lynch talk, and your brother took it in his head to interfere." He gave Farley Ingram a dark scowl. "It's been a hard job to get him riled at that outfit, and then he goes and blows up over a thing that didn't even matter!"

"A man's life matters," Ingram retorted, feeling the warmth that spread into his cheeks. "Anyway, it's done and over with. Right now, I think we better be getting after Mort's cattle before it scatters in the timber."

"That's a sound thought," Mort Woods agreed. "And the mood Hatchet's in, if they should double back on us I wouldn't like to be caught in the open!" He slid his rifle into the scabbard and barked an order at his riders. The group put their horses onto the chopped-up trail the jag of beef had left.

Luckily, the stock hadn't scattered badly. The riders quickly picked them up, moving in on the flank and rear and shaping them into a drive again, starting them once more through the wet columns of the trees. A short mile farther on, where the trail entered a tiny pocket meadow was the place to make their stand if there had to be one. They found it brightly green with new grass and Woods's riders let the cattle spill onto this, holding them close enough that they could be put quickly into motion again if need be. The other three dismounted, tied their horses, and hastily took up positions commanding the backtrail.

Shoulder against the wet trunk of a thick pine, rifle barrel chill in his hands, Farley Ingram listened to the stir of the feeding cattle and the whisper of rain in the branches overhead and waited tensely for the first sound that would warn of the Hatchet crew coming after them. Yonder, he could see his younger brother hugging the shadow of another tree and grinning with excitement. He shook his head, sorely troubled. Only a kid as green and ignorant as Bob could find anything pleasurable in this. Bob was spoiling for a fight. To him, the idea of an open clash with Hatchet seemed like great sport; and though Ingram trembled for him there was really nothing he could do.

The boy wouldn't believe what he didn't learn for himself, and he was too near grown now for his brother to give him orders and make them stick. At that age, a kid had to be handled with an easy rein or he got hard-jawed and completely unmanageable. Thus, today, Farley Ingram had known it would only blow up a row if he made any real effort to keep him at the ranch, instead of letting him help Mort Woods move this bunch, despite the fact they had all known it meant risking the open breach with Hatchet that, if possible, anybody with mature sense would have wanted to avert.

A peaceful man, having the intelligence and the imagination to visualize what war could mean, Farley Ingram wanted to avoid it at nearly any cost. It saddened him to know that, as a result, his young hawk of a brother looked on him with a certain amount of contempt. But, someone had to use his head.

Only, for that matter, he hadn't done too well himself, interfering in the matter of the drifter, and old man Hardman's stolen claybank! What kind of a way had *that* been, of avoiding the clash he feared with Hatchet?

He realized that, as he stood here grappling with his moody thoughts, time had been slipping by with no hint of trouble approaching along the drive trail through the trees. Now Mort Woods came toward him, moving with that forthright prowl that was characteristic of the man. He stopped beside Ingram, waggling the rifle he held by the balance, his puzzled scowl showing he was beginning to entertain the same thought that was nagging the other man.

"No sign of Hatchet," he said bluntly. "I don't think they're even coming."

"I kind of thought they'd be here, if they were," Farley Ingram admitted. "So it begins to look as though they're less interested in your beef, than in catching up that fellow with the claybank."

"I don't understand it! We run this stuff past their noses and they let them go by as if they didn't so much as notice!"

Bob had come up in time to hear this. He showed all his strong white teeth. "We scared 'em off! We proved we didn't give a hoot in hell about their deadline, and they backed down!"

"Don't be fool enough to believe that!" his brother snapped. "We maybe caught Russ Quint off guard, but we never scared him. We could never have disarmed them without a fight. A standoff was the best we could manage, and Quint decided for reasons of his own to let us get away with it."

"But the deadline!" Mort Woods insisted. "How can they make it stick, if they let us get away with crossing it the first time anyone had the nerve to try? Is catching some tramp horse thief more important to them than a bid to control the whole Valley?"

Farley Ingram took his time answering. He turned to where his horse stood tied to a branch, slid the rifle into the saddle boot and then stood a moment with a hand on the bronc's shoulder. "I'll tell you the truth," he said finally. "It isn't the first time I've wondered — could it be there never *was* a deadline?"

Mort Woods stared at him. "Don't try to tell me this was nothing but a *bluff!* When Coleman Dorsey passed the word about Hatchet taking back all the summer grass on this east side of the Colton he wasn't doing it just to hear himself talk. Not Cole Dorsey!"

"But are we sure he really said it?"

"Hell! Everybody in the Valley knows . . ."

"Everybody knows what somebody else told him," Ingram pointed out, patiently. "But have you talked to anyone who actually heard Dorsey, or old man Hardman, or any other Hatchet man warn him to stay off the hills? Think about it."

The 3W rancher scowled, started to speak and then hesitated, while young Bob looked blankly from one to the other. Finally Woods blurted, "Even rumor has to start somewhere!"

"It can sometimes start with fear," Ingram reminded him, "with the general mood of uneasiness that's been heavy on this range while we all wondered just what Hatchet was up to. Maybe somebody said,

'What are we gonna do if they decide to close us out of our summer grass?' And maybe somebody misheard him and passed the word along — 'Hatchet's giving warning for the rest of us to keep out of the hills.' And it went on building from there. It could happen that way."

"Then you think we've all let ourselves get worked up over nothing?" Woods sounded heavily skeptical. "And all them heavy guns that Coleman Dorsey's been putting on the payroll, they're for no reason?"

"If you didn't have doubts about the deadline," the other pointed out, "why were you ready to risk testing them by pushing this bunch across it?"

"Because I was desperate, that's why! Hell! We can't none of us function without our summer range, any fool knows that. Hand it over, without a murmur, and we'll have no option but to move out and let Hatchet take everything. And yet, you two were the only ones who seemed willing to throw in with me and the boys, at the risk of a fight. Was that because you didn't actually think there'd be one?"

"I was hoping," Farley Ingram admitted. "It's been a long time since there was any real trouble with Hatchet, six years, at least. I just hated to think it could be starting again, now."

His brother, who had been listening to all this without comment, broke in suddenly. "Well, if you're right, then what are we standing around talking for?" He flushed slightly as the older men turned to look at him, but he persisted, facing his brother, "I mean, we got us a herd of our own, that we been holding too long already on winter pasture. If there's nothing to stop us from moving 'em, we ought to be getting at it before they all starve to death on us. That is, assumin' you really believe what you been telling us!"

Ingram looked at the young fellow, gauging his impetuous recklessness. Even as he hesitated, he thought he saw an answer to a problem that had been bothering him. "You know," he said judiciously, "you got a good point there, kid."

He glanced at the weeping sky. "This day's far gone, but there just may be time to get our stuff bunched and ready to move out tomorrow. Why don't you go down, and you and Willie Ryker pull 'em together on the south pasture and hold them. I'll stay here and help Mort and his boys get this 3W bunch settled. Come morning, if there's still been no trouble from Hatchet, then the two of you start movin' 'em, and I'll drop down to meet you and lend a hand."

Bob agreed eagerly. "Now you're making sense." he cried. "We'll show Quint, and Coleman Dorsey, and Hardman and all the rest, just how scared the Ingrams are of any deadline!" He turned and hurried to his horse, almost running. Ripping the reins loose from where he had anchored them to a pine branch stub, he flung himself into the saddle with an ease that made his older brother wince, feeling his own years in the ache that a day's riding put across his lower back.

Riding over to look down at the other pair from the back of his sorrel, Bob reined in long enough to say, "I'll see you in the morning then, with the whole damn Ingram herd!" He answered his brother's nod with the wave of a hand, and immediately wrenched his animal about and spurred him into the hoof-chopped trail leading back down to the valley floor. They listened until the sound of his going was absorbed by the muddy earth, and the timber, and the whisper of the rain.

Mort Woods cocked a look at Farley Ingram. "He never guessed, did he?" And as the other frowned at him, "Hell! You

71

don't fool me. You damn well think we *could* still get a fight here, and you don't want Bob in it."

Ingram lifted a shoulder inside his wetly shining slicker. He said, "If I could have prevented it, he'd never have come up with us today. He's just a kid. Trouble is, he's got too big for me to boss around any more, like I once could.

"I admit I don't know what to expect from Hatchet, before this day's out. There's still plenty of time left for trouble — and I'm going to feel a hell of a lot better, knowing I don't have to worry about him being in it."

Chapter 6

A jackrabbit, making off through the sage in a gray streak sent Bob Ingram to fumbling for his holster. He got the gun out and managed to thumb off a couple of shots, with absolutely no effect at all. The jack zigzagged ahead and out of sight, the mingled echoes of the shots bounced away and were swallowed up by the cloud-swollen sky. Bob only grinned and shoved the gun back into the holster, afterward speaking to settle his horse that had shied a bit in protest.

Pure elation and a tingling excitement had made it hard to sit still in the saddle, or hold to a careful gait as he made his way down from the hills. Now, as he struck the flats and dropped into an easy trail leading directly toward the home ranch, he let the sorrel out and sent it drumming over the soggy earth at a pace that matched his mood; the wind flattened the hatbrim against his forehead and tore the gleeful war whoop from his lips and scattered it.

He drew in, presently, on a rise that gave

him a view of the town of Colton lying over to his left, amid a scatter of cotton-woods along the creek bottom that were beginning to leaf out well as spring advanced. While the horse blew and stamped under him, Bob Ingram rubbed a palm across his rain-wet cheeks and considered. Naturally, he was eager to get home and get a start, with Willie Ryker, at bunching the herd for tomorrow's drive up to the hills; still, it would only be a couple of miles out of the way if he were to drop into town first. Of course, he couldn't really claim to have business there. . . .

Then a happy thought occurred to him. This was Tuesday and no one had been in yet for the week's mail. That was perfectly sound reasoning, and all the excuse he needed. In another moment he had swung his bridles into the trail fork that led on down to the heart of the valley, and the scatter of homes and business houses that made up the town of Colton.

It was drab enough at any time, and the rain made it dreary. The wide street slick with mud, pocked with standing puddles that reflected the dull cloud ceiling, the unpainted buildings weathered to a uniform gray. The creek, which he crossed on a plank bridge, gleamed like dull pewter, freckled by the rain. There was hardly anyone abroad. Bob Ingram rode directly to Olland's Mercantile, where he left his horse at the tie bar and stepped up onto the porch, ducking a twisted rope of rainwater that runneled noisily off the overhang. A bell on a spring above the door jangled as he entered.

Bob pulled off his hat and shook some of the water from it, swiped it once against the front of his yellow slicker. He combed his hair with blunt fingers, looking about the gloomy interior with its bins and counters and tiers of shelves piled with an indiscriminate jumble of goods.

Now Margie Olland entered through a rear door, answering the summons of the bell. Bob grinned at the sight of her. She was a small girl, about his own age, blonde and rather thin. She was not particularly pretty, the paleness of her features matched by the nearly invisible brows and lashes, but young Bob Ingram thought her beautiful. The top of her head came barely to a level with his own chin; she seemed to him delicately and extraordinarily made, and in her presence he was always conscious of his own awkwardness and the size of his hands and feet.

"Hi," he said, and then, remembering

the excuse he had allowed himself, "I dropped in to get the mail."

It would help, he sometimes thought, if he could ever be sure what she was thinking, whether she really liked him, or not. But a girl's mind was unfamiliar territory to Bob Ingram, and this girl was so very quiet and held so much in reserve that he never knew if she was only shy or actually disapproved of him. She didn't even smile at him now, as she might have been expected to for even a casual customer. She looked at him briefly and her glance dropped from his and she said, almost coldly, "I don't think there was anything this time. Maybe a couple of catalogues. I'll look."

He switched his weight from one boot to the other, uncomfortably, while she went behind the counter to the grilled window that served Colton Valley for a post office. Briefly rummaging, Margie found a saddlemaker's catalogue and a couple of issues of a stockman's journal which Bob took and shoved into a pocket. Afterward they stood and looked at each other; he cleared his throat and asked, "How have you all been?"

"I'm fine," she said. "Uncle Gil is fine." She hesitated. "We haven't seen much of you lately."

It was all the encouragement he needed. "This is the busy time of year. We had a good calf drop. Got 'em all branded, and now we got our herd to shove up onto summer pasture." He spoke offhandedly, watching for her reaction, and was rewarded as her eyes widened behind their pale lashes. She stared.

"Summer pasture?" she echoed. "But you can't! I mean, I heard . . ."

"I guess I know what you heard," Bob interrupted airily. "That Hatchet's decided to go back to the tactics it was using a few years ago, when old man Hardman seemed bent on squeezing every other ranch out of the Valley and leaving his the only spread, like in the beginning. And I guess you heard they was planning to start by taking all our summer range." He shrugged. "You didn't suppose me and Farley would stand still for any such bluff as that, did you?"

Margie Olland shook her head a little. "I, I don't know," she exclaimed vaguely.

"Well, if Hatchet thought so they sure found out different, today! You know what we just got through doing? We run some stuff up across the deadline they tried to set, right under Russ Quint's nose. And he couldn't do a damn thing to stop us!"

"You mean, there was a fight?"

"It come pretty close to one," Bob said. "Sid Tacker and some of the others with him really wanted to burn powder. But they never had a chance when I drew a bead on Quint. You should have seen him! He knew he was a dead man if he tried anything, all right. So in the end he hadn't no choice but to call off his wolves, and leave us alone to do what we come for."

The girl's blue eyes held on his face. Her own cheeks were drained of color. "*You* put a gun on Russ Quint?" He thought her voice had a tremor in it, and a warm glow sprang to life inside him. He made a modest gesture.

"I probably wouldn't have *killed* him," he explained. "Not unless he really crowded me. But of course, Quint had no way of knowing that, and so you can't blame him for being cautious. It wasn't like he was yellow, or anything!" Bob pushed away from the counter where he had been leaning as he talked, enjoying the astonishment and concern that he saw in Margie's stare.

"Well, I got to be traveling. That was Mort Woods's stuff we took up there today," he went on, hardly aware that he had forgotten to mention the fact that Mort and his two hands had been along, or had had anything to do with it. "Tomorrow, Willie Ryker and me will be throwing our own stuff onto our usual summer grass, up under Hat Butte. So, there's a lot to do."

"You be careful, Bob Ingram!"

He made a gesture with one hand. "I reckon we can handle anything that needs it." Still he was troubled by a vague feeling that he might have said a trifle too much. He hesitated and then suggested, in a tone he tried to make sound as though the request was not really too important, "Maybe, though, you might just keep this to yourself, for the time being anyway. I ain't one for crowing, just because I made Russ Quint back water. And as for moving our herd tomorrow morning, well, I reckon that's me and Farley's business. The whole valley don't need to know."

Reluctant to end this pleasant conversation, he couldn't leave without seizing the chance to suggest, "There's a dance next Saturday. You fixing to go? I mean, would you like to go with me, maybe?"

"Well —" It was disappointing to see the way she hesitated. He had begun to believe she would jump at the chance, but she looked down at the hands knotted together in front of her, and all he could see of her face was the pale line of her cheek and the neat center part in her blond hair. She looked up then but seemed to have trouble with her answer. "I'll have to see what Uncle Gil says. He might want me here in the store that evening. . . ."

"O.K., O.K.," Bob Ingram said gruffly. "I'll check with you later, huh?" But his mood was badly soured as he turned and tramped outside to his horse.

He couldn't help the nagging thought that he might have said too much, about things his brother Farley would have wanted him to keep to himself.

In the dark storage space behind the rear partition, Gil Olland stood with a heavy case of tin goods forgotten in his hands for a long minute after the door closed, and listened to the echoes of the bell jangle into silence through the big store building. The things he had heard drew his mouth out into a long scowl and set the muscles at the hinges of his jaw to fluttering.

He was a small man, fine-boned, and as blond as Margie who looked enough like him to be taken for a daughter instead of his niece. The years since his first coming to the valley had thinned his hair, added rimless spectacles to weakened blue eyes and rounded his shoulders with toil; they'd also shortened his tolerance for the changes he saw more and more around him. To him, the Valley meant Hatchet. It was Nat Hardman himself, after all, who had found him and encouraged him to come here and open a store — had practically built it for him, out of his own pocket, simply because he considered the town of Colton had need of one.

And so, although he told himself he wished no man harm, Gil Olland found it hard to tolerate upstarts who crowded in to whittle away at range that had always been Hatchet. Nat Hardman had been too lenient, for too long. There was a time, a few years back, when it had looked like he meant to take positive action; but after his wife died suddenly, Nat appeared to have lost something of his fire, and gone soft toward the encroachments of his neighbors. Well, it was good to see a firmer stand being taken, at last.

Just as, by God, Gil Olland was going to have to take a firmer stand with nobodies like that Bob Ingram youngster! He and his brother never seemed able to keep their bill paid, from one year's end to the other, and it was plain they had nothing and never would make anything of that hardscrabble, two-bit ranch of theirs. And yet the kid had gall enough to come sniffing around and impressing Margie with all his empty talk.

Shaking his head, still scowling to himself, Olland remembered the heavy weight in his hands and walked out onto the loading platform at the back of the store. A ranch wagon stood backed up to it. Nels McPhee, one of Hatchet's hands, leaned against the wagon, trying to keep a cigarette burning despite the drizzling rain. He slanted a look at the storekeeper through the smoke. "You took your time fetching that!" he grunted. "What's the idea, keeping me waiting out here?"

Olland leaned to set the case into the wagon bed and McPhee gave it a shove forward to better place the weight. He fastened the tailgate and was about to turn away when Olland, squatting on the edge of the platform, called him back. McPhee, a tough, blackhaired man with a damaged and drooping eyelid, looked up at him from the ground. "Well?"

Olland swallowed, then told it fast. "I just heard that Ingram kid talking big in front of my niece. He said they're moving their cattle up to Hat Butte in the morning."

The other's look sharpened. "The hell they are!"

"I'm just telling you what he said. I

thought Nat or Mister Dorsey might want to know."

Nels McPhee studied him closely for a long moment. Then he took the soggy butt from his lips, looked to see if it was worth relighting, and instead flung it into the mud. "All right," he said, and nothing more. He swung away and hitched himself up onto the wagon's seat, took the leather, kicked off the brake.

Gil Olland, straightening to a stand, frowned as he watched him ride away along the mud-deep alley, through the rain.

It wasn't a heavy rain, but as the long afternoon drew on, a sharp wind had come up to fling it at a man like so many needling spears, that could torment his face and work its way though nearly any clothing. Jim Bannister, without hat or slicker or gun, on a horse that didn't belong to him, felt by now that he could indeed pass for the thing he had been called more than once today, a range tramp, in a borrowed saddle, soaked to the hide and without destination and without hope.

He supposed that if that was the worst people here thought of him, it was far better than having them guess the truth.

He could still make little sense of the matters he had stumbled into since crossing the pass over the toll road this morning. There were confused currents of hatred and violence — men here were at cross purposes, as men were everywhere else, but what sides were drawn, and who was on them, was more than he had been able to sort out. Actually, of course, none of it was his affair, except for one fact that he couldn't get past: a hurt man, lying in a hole under a rimrock, with no one but Jim Bannister to help him if by this time he wasn't already dead.

Bannister still didn't know these hills; to ride through them blind could mean blundering again into Russ Quint's hands, or, what would be even worse, leading him straight to Hardman's hiding place. He hadn't the slightest idea that Quint had given up. For whatever reason, those Hatchet riders had just one thing on their minds: finding the owner of the claybank and killing him.

For all Bannister knew, they could be watching his every move at this very moment. In the end, he had to settle for pretending to be the range tramp everyone seemed to take him for. He went drifting aimlessly down through the timber toward lower country, trying to behave, for the benefit of any observer, as though there were no definite purpose in his mind.

The valley wall dropped away rather abruptly onto rolling benchland, well grassed and watered and timbered sparsely with scattered pine and some aspen thickets. Riding over this, he had occasional glimpses of the bottomland still below him, and the steely glint that would be Colton Creek itself. Good range, he thought, the kind of country, unfortunately, that all too often turned men greedy.

It was a reasonable guess that greed lay at the bottom of the trouble he saw taking shape here. It seemed to lie at the root of most kinds of trouble, as Bannister had reason to know. After all, an Eastern syndicate's greed for his own New Mexico horse course, none of was his affair, except for one fact death of his wife and setting him adrift with an unjust conviction of murder hanging over his head. Riding down now through this Colorado hill country, he found himself wondering if men really deserved such a magnificent place to live in. Too many of them were selfish brutes who destroyed the land, without ever noticing the beauty they ravaged.

The rain continued intermittently, though the clouds seemed to be thinning a little; the sun was faintly visible now, as a greasy smear against the gray ceiling. Bannister could not shake a feeling that he was being observed, though he could detect no sign of another rider than himself. Presently he hauled rein within the windbreak of a clump of rock to dig out the materials he'd bought from Wolford, and try to fire up a cigarette.

Chill damp had managed to work into the paper and tobacco sack, even inside his shirt pocket, but he managed to get one put together. Taking out a match, he was about to strike it on his thumbnail when movement on a ridge, just above and to the right of where he sat, brought his head around sharply. It was a man on horseback, a shapeless figure in the bulky rubber slicker and high-crowned range hat, sitting motionless where only a moment ago, Bannister was certain, there had been only the empty ridgeline.

Shaken, he made himself snap the match alight and deliberately applied it to the twisted end of the cigarette in his mouth, taking his time, as though getting the damp paper to burning was his only concern. When he had it done and the first plume of smoke streamed from his lips, he blew out the match and flipped it aside and at the same time sneaked another look.

The rider was still there.

Mouth grim, Bannister picked up the reins. There wasn't much doubt in his mind that the man on the ridge intended to be seen, his silent presence meant for a warning. Hard to tell at this distance, but Bannister was convinced he must be one of Russ Quint's men. Now the rider started forward, and before he was swallowed up in the brush that shagged the hillside, Bannister clearly saw the rifle he carried in one hand.

He could have picked Bannister off with it easily. He meant that to be known, too.

Jim Bannister swore, and rode on.

He had intended taking a route that would lead around the break off of the ridge; now instead, to avoid a meeting he had to swing to the left. That meant picking his way down the steep and crumbling bank of a rocky streambed, and finding another place opposite where the claybank could climb out again. He crossed a stony hump of ground, where a jackstraw tangle of blowndown timber made rough going. Minutes after clearing that, he entered a sloping meadow that was crisscrossed by stock trails. Half way over it he turned in the saddle, he saw that a second horseman had joined the first and they were both coming on at an easy walk, half a mile behind him.

Apparently they thought he might decide to cut away toward the timber at the head of the meadow, for now one of them split off and began circling in that direction. Seeing that, Bannister finally knew what was happening. They were deliberately driving him, herding him the way they wanted him to go. At the thought a surge of rebellion went through him, leaving him trembling with anger; but that was useless. He was unarmed, and they knew it. Nor could he run from them because he doubted the claybank had any run left in it. It had been working hard, without letup, in tough country; and while he couldn't be sure that Quint's animals were fresher, he didn't have the heart to push the claybank in what would likely prove a futile chase at best.

So, he decided bleakly, he would just see what it was they wanted of him.

A half hour later, down nearly onto the rolling valley floor, he dropped into a plainly marked wagon road. With a choice of two ways to go, he reined in and turned to face his drivers, frankly waiting for an indication. There were three riders by this time and he was sure he recognized Sid Tacker among them, though they had been keeping their distance and making no move to overtake or hurry him. Now, still without haste, one spurred his horse at an angle to the left as though intending to cut off the road in that direction.

It was all the hint Bannister needed. He actually raised an arm in mocking acknowledgment before swinging the claybank to the right. The wagon road made easier going and he lifted to a half canter. Looking back he saw that the others, too, had increased their pace accordingly.

Presently a fence line showed ahead, posts strung with dully gleaming wire. The road passed it through an open gate; from the high cross bar a wooden sign hung and swayed, creaking faintly in the rain-wet wind. Coming under it Bannister could see a brand burnt into the panel, a few deft strokes with a running iron, making the design that resembled an Indian tomahawk.

"Hatchet," he said aloud. And then, addressing the trio of riders still hanging back a couple of hundred yards to his rear,

"All right, damn you, I'm willing. Let's get some matters straightened out!"

He touched the spur to his borrowed horse and sent it under the arch, toward a complex of buildings and corrals that he could see, through the rain, in a pocket of the ground a mile ahead. And at once the pursuing horsemen lifted their mounts and began to close the distance.

Chapter 7

Lamps were already burning in a couple of the buildings, with an early dusk not too far from settling on this raw, dark day. Now, too, the jaded claybank pricked its ears and got a little spring into its gait, indicating clearly enough, even without the brand it bore, that home and feed and a dry stall lay just beyond. Bannister let it have its head, while he put his attention on the ranch layout.

It was a good-sized spread, and it had been there for some time. There were two bunkhouses, the original having been outgrown as the ranch expanded; the newer and larger one had a messroom and kitchen tacked onto one end. The hay barn was spacious, the battery of corrals adequate for a large crew. Sitting apart from the rest, with a windscreen of tall poplars planted around three sides of it, the main house was partly log and partly stone, and appeared to have been added to as time required.

There were a dozen head of goodlooking horses running in one of the corrals. Now, riding in through the rain, Bannister saw another animal standing under saddle at the tie rail that fronted the veranda of the house, where lampglow showed behind a curtained window. The horse was a big roan that seemed familiar even before he had got close enough for a better look and recognized it.

Russ Quint had been riding that horse when he and his men captured Jim Bannister in the hills.

It shouldn't have been unexpected, but it came as rather a shock to know the man was here ahead of him. Involuntarily Bannister reined in, and looked behind him to see Tacker and the other pair coming up. They had spread out some as they rode into the yard; their slickers gleamed faintly and so did the barrel of the gun in Sid Tacker's hand. As Bannister halted so did they. The thin rain made a pelting noise on the mud; wet wind lashed the poplars that were still only beginning to leaf out.

Tacker lifted the gun. "You're doing fine," he told Bannister with heavy humor. "Don't stop now. Just light down, and tie."

Without a word Bannister put the tired claybank to the rail beside Quint's chestnut, and stepped stiffly from the saddle. As he was tying, with the loose wrap of the leather that would hold a trained cowhorse to the tooth-marked pole, Tacker swung down and tossed his reins to one of the others. His gun covered the prisoner while the other horses were put to the rail, bracketing the two that were already there. After that, a jerk of the gunbarrel pointed Bannister toward the steps and he turned to mount them, with the Hatchet riders closing in behind.

Just as they gained the veranda, the door was suddenly thrown open and Russ Quint's blocky shape filled it. When he saw the prisoner he stared, and gave a short grunt of satisfaction. "Well, by God!" Abruptly he stepped back and threw the door wide; a hand was laid on Bannister's shoulder from behind and pushed him roughly. He walked through the door, past Quint, and the rest followed hard after.

Even in a first glance, this was an attractive and comfortable room with exposed beams in the low ceiling overhead and polished boards and scattered throw rugs underfoot. There was evidence of a woman's touch — curtains at the window, brightly colored cushions on the pair of sofas flanking the stone fireplace where a log burned. Spring flowers, in bowls set here and there about the room, combatted the dullness of the rainy afternoon.

A man sat on one of the sofas, his face hidden behind the stockman's journal he was reading by the light of a lamp on the table beside him. Bannister was marched before this man and brought to a stand, while they all waited in patient silence; obviously the man was not to be interrupted in his reading by a mere hired hand. It was only when he moved to turn a page that Russ Quint cleared his throat and said respectfully, "Mister Dorsey, this is him. This here's the son of a bitch that give us the trouble. The boys just brung him in."

The paper was lowered. Jim Bannister looked into the face, and the cold gray eyes, of the one who had shown such a peculiar interest in him that morning, up at the toll house.

Deliberately, without taking his studying glance from the prisoner, Coleman Dorsey folded the paper and laid it on the sofa beside him. "Well?" he said finally. "Has he talked yet?"

Russ Quint looked at Tacker for the answer; the redhead grunted. "We didn't ask any more questions, we only brung him. Damn range tramp!"

"That's as may be; I'm not so sure. He

came through Wolford's gate this morning,"
Coleman Dorsey said, his stare searching
the stranger's face. "He looked considerably different then. In fact," he told Quint,
"I thought he might be someone you had
hired."

"Not me," Quint answered flatly. "He's
nobody at all *I* know."

The other nodded. "So I concluded. I
gave him a chance but he didn't act as
though he wanted to speak to me. Showed
no sign of even knowing who I was." He
slapped both hands upon his knees, and
came off the sofa with an easy movement.

Like the other Hatchet men, he stood a
bit shorter than their prisoner; but as he
faced Bannister there was something about
his bearing that appeared to lessen the difference in their heights. His eyes were
completely cold as he said, not angrily,
"The boys tell me you think you are a
pretty tough fellow. Just what do you hope
to gain by continuing to hold out on us?"

Jim Bannister shrugged. It seemed as
good an answer as any.

At once Sid Tacker, standing behind
him, dealt him a cunning blow against a
kidney, a hard-knuckled punch that filled
him with pain and caused his knees to sag.
Bannister caught himself, and as through a

red haze saw Quint and Dorsey eyeing him. The latter promised, "You're going to talk eventually, you know. You're only being tough on yourself."

Face expressionless, holding himself erect with an effort, Bannister returned the stare. Behind him Tacker cursed softly.

Coleman Dorsey said, "Let's try again. Where did you leave Hardman?"

"I don't know any Hardman," Jim Bannister lied.

He knew what was coming this time, and was ready for it when Tacker jabbed him again. Despite the hurting ache throughout his body he turned with the blow, letting it graze him and draw Tacker off balance. Before anyone guessed his intent, his own fist sank into the redhead's middle. The man doubled forward, the wind exploding from his lips. As Tacker staggered back, Bannister tensed himself for a bullet or a blow from a gunbarrel, but Dorsey stopped his men before any of them could retaliate.

"All right! *All right!*" he said sharply. And to Bannister, "You really ask for it, don't you?"

"I told you he was tough, Cole," Russ Quint reminded him.

By now Sid Tacker had managed to get

part of his wind back. Face red with fury, he wheezed out between gasps, "I'll kill him!" Bannister thought surely he would grab up the gun from his holster and do it, then and there.

Coleman Dorsey, however, ignored the redhead. Studying Bannister with those chill gray eyes he asked, "Do you have a name?"

The prisoner said, "You're not interested in my name."

"You're right," Dorsey said, nodding. "I'm only interested in where you got the claybank. If you won't tell me that, then you're no use to me. I might as well turn you over to Sid Tacker and let him finish you off, since he wants to so much."

And if I do tell you, Bannister thought, *you'll kill me anyway!* There was no choice, so he kept his mouth shut and waited, defiantly, and he hoped with a greater show of self confidence than he was actually feeling. Standing there surrounded by his enemies, he wondered if this was really the end of the road.

Then one of the men grunted a warning and Coleman Dorsey, turning quickly, scowled at the hall doorway. The woman who had been with him at the toll house that morning stood there, silently watching.

She had changed her traveling costume for a simple house dress, but Bannister saw at once the difference was in the pallor, and the look of deep anxiety, that were visible on her pretty face. She said uncertainly, "I thought I heard voices. Have you learned something about . . . ?"

"No," Coleman Dorsey interrupted curtly, crossing to her. At the moment, Bannister sucked in his breath as he felt the hard round pressure of a gunmuzzle come against his back, a warning, to hold him where he was and keep him still.

Dorsey loomed over the woman and placed a hand on her shoulder. He spoke impatiently, as he might to a child: "There's still nothing. Some of the boys were just checking in. They're doing their best. Didn't I say I'd tell you as soon as I had news?"

She looked anxiously up into his face, and then beyond him at the knot of waiting men who stood dripping rainwater from yellow slickers and soaked clothing. It was doubtful that she even registered their faces.

Now she turned again to Coleman Dorsey, who continued talking in a lowered voice; only an occasional word carried above the snap and roar of the log burning in the fireplace. Jim Bannister was conscious of its welcome warmth beginning to have some effect; a smell of steaming wool mingled with the scent of pinesmoke.

Someone shifted his boots, impatiently. And suddenly it occurred to the prisoner that there could be an opportunity here, if he had the nerve to risk it.

He drew a breath.

"We're burning daylight," he said loudly, to no one in particular. "One thing's clear, we'll never get anywhere, if we stand here talking. I'm hitting the saddle again." And he turned boldly toward the exit.

He met startled stares, and a mouth or two that had fallen open in the face of such audacity. Sid Tacker made as though to seize his arm, but in passing, Bannister surreptitiously rammed an elbow that made the redhead fall back a step. Then there was no one between him and the door that looked about a mile away. He kept walking, tensed for the moment when those others got over their first surprise and moved to stop him.

But he had a hunch, and was gambling on it, that the presence of the woman would somehow keep them from an overt move. It began to look as though his hunch was correct. The distance between himself and freedom shrank with each deliberate step, and still no sound or interference came from behind. And now he reached his goal; his hand fell on the knob.

As the door swung open, Cole Dorsey spoke in a voice that, to Bannister's acute senses, appeared to hold a tremor of barely disguised rage, "Well, Sid? What are the rest of you going to do?"

Bannister pulled the door shut on that, knowing Dorsey's words would be the signal to free the others from their tracks. Instantly he was across the veranda, at a single stride, and leaping the short drop to the ground. Five saddled horses, one of them Nat Hardman's claybank, made a shoulder-to-shoulder lineup along the hitchrail. He rounded an end of it and frantically began grabbing reins. The middle horse in the line was Quint's which had been there longest and was probably the best rested; hampered by the imprisoned leathers, Bannister flung himself onto the roan's saddle and sent it lunging hard against the claybank, next to it.

The latter tried to back free of the pole; this stretched its reins and made it easier to reach and grab them and tug the slipknot loose. The last horse had been more securely tied and gave him trouble, so that for a moment he thought he would have to leave it. But just as the big door burst open and men came spilling out upon the veranda, a final jerk at the knot whipped it free.

Someone on the veranda let out a yell but, with plenty to occupy him, trying to manage four extra horses as well as the one between his knees, he did not even look that way. Luckily, the roan responded well to the reins and to the spur. It shouldered the two animals on its near side out of the way, and now Bannister was somehow able to get all five horses turned from the hitch rail. At once he booted the roan into a run, towing the rest on their leathers, two on either flank, their hoofs drumming up thunder from the soggy earth.

He was gambling again, on the thin chance his enemies would be reluctant to shoot at their own horses, or give Coleman Dorsey more to explain to the woman in the house. It seemed a poor enough bet, but so far no gun had sounded behind him, no bullet followed him as he crouched low to make a smaller target.

The roan slipped once in the yard's greasy mud and missed stride, and for a heart-stopping moment Bannister thought it was going to bring him down in a grand pile-up of horseflesh and flailing shoe irons. But it caught its footing and ran on, and the others ran with it. Now Bannister did glance back, to see the dark figures of men making a dash through the rain, from house to corral. It probably would not take them long to catch up fresh horses, but the delay had won him a precious start.

He still could scarcely believe it.

When the ranch buildings had been lost behind a fold in the land, he risked halting long enough to sort out the double fistfuls of leather that hampered him. In the end he kept only Quint's horse, which he was riding, and Sid Tacker's chestnut, the sturdiest of the lot. The rest, including Nat Hardman's badly jaded claybank, he cast adrift. Riding on, he thought with grim irony that he was now, many times over, the horse thief the Hatchet men had called him! Well, it had gained him his purpose of holding up pursuit for the time it would take his enemies to catch and saddle. Encumbered now with only one extra mount, he was already making better time as he spurred under the crossbar of the high gateway.

It was raining hard again, coming down in silver sheets and beating hard upon his unprotected head and body. For all his discomfort, Jim Bannister was glad to see this and to see that premature dusk was settling, leaking daylight out of the cloud-tumbled sky. Steady rain and darkness would be his greatest allies in trying to lose pursuit. He pointed for the nearest timber and drove his horses toward it; just before entering the dark belt of pines, he looked back and saw a clump of riders. He counted a half dozen, and then the trees closed about him.

Here, in the timber, night seemed very close. But he kept pushing the horses as hard as he dared, and presently reined in while he switched over to the saddle of Sid Tacker's chestnut and cast the roan loose, first hooking the reins over the saddlehorn so that it could make its way back to Hatchet and not get hung up in the brush. Then he had a thought which set him digging into Tacker's saddlebag pockets. Sure enough, his gun that the redhead had taken from him, was still there. There was a carbine, too, in the saddle boot. When he had checked his handgun and replaced it in its holster, Jim Bannister felt considerably more optimistic.

He listened but heard no sound more threatening than the whisper of rain in treeheads and brush around him, but perhaps this only masked the approach of his enemies. He had a feeling they would not be letting up on him until the fast-nearing fall of night made searching hopeless.

Bannister nudged the chestnut with the spur, and rode on into a rainy dusk.

Russ Quint followed out onto the veranda in time to see Tacker sighting down his gunarm, for a revolver shot after the dwindling shape of the fugitive. Quint swore and slapped the arm down, saying harshly, "Damn it, you know Cole wants no shooting here. Not with *her* around!"

The redhead turned on him, ruddy face made even redder by the fury that shook him. "By God, I'll kill the bastard! No range tramp lays a hand on me!" He still rankled, plainly, over the belly blow that had knocked the wind from him.

"You'll have to catch him first." Quint said bluntly, and indicated the others who were already splashing off toward the holding corral and fresh horses. "Go along with them. And if there's anyone in the bunkhouse, clean 'em out. Damn it, get after him!"

Tacker mumbled something but was on his way, fumbling to holster his gun as he ran with the slicker swishing about his legs.

Staying where he was, Quint scowled and slapped one rope-hardened palm against the railing as Coleman Dorsey came out to join him. "They'll never catch him now," the range boss said bluntly.

They watched the Hatchet crew go streaming out of the yard on hastily saddled animals. "And we're still no closer than we ever were," Dorsey pointed out, "to knowing who or what he is. I take it you never thought to search the man while you had him."

"No." A warm flush crept up over Quint's cheeks as he admitted it. "It just didn't occur to me. It seemed so obvious he was a nobody, a thievin' range tramp."

"Well, we know now that, whatever he is, he isn't *that!* Not the man who had enough cool nerve to know we'd let him bluff his way out of that house, rather than risk a scene in front of her."

Quint said anxiously, "Do you think she suspected anything?"

"Not really."

They were silent a long moment, staring into the gathering gloom. Finally Russ Quint asked, "Where do you suppose the bastard's headed now?"

"It should be obvious. He's got the old man hid out somewhere, while he took the claybank and led you off his trail. He'll be going back there, soon as he figures it's safe. And the hell of it is, he knows Tacker and the rest haven't any real chance of catching him."

They were contemplating this when the sound of an approaching wagon and team came through the rainy evening. Presently the vehicle rolled into the yard and pulled to a halt before the house. The driver was Nels McPhee, a puncher Quint had sent to town on errands earlier in the day. He called up to the pair that was dimly visible in the shadows of the veranda: "Boss? That you? I got news."

"Come on up." McPhee swung quickly off the wagon, leaving his team standing, and hurriedly took the steps. Dorsey sensed an urgency in him. "Something wrong in town?"

"I just heard some news," the puncher said again. "From Gil Olland."

"The storekeeper. Well?"

"He told me he done heard his niece talkin' to the Ingram kid, that younger one."

Russ Quint supplied the name. "Bob."

"I reckon. Anyway, it looks like they're fixing to move their herd onto summer grass, under Hat Butte. According to

Olland, they'll be moving 'em up to-morrow, early. He said the kid sounded boastful, told the gal they'd helped run a bunch of Mort Woods's stuff across the deadline today, right under Quint's nose, and now they're planning to follow it with their own beef."

"So?" And Coleman Dorsey turned and stared hard at the range boss, while rain drummed on roof shingles above their heads.

Stung, Russ Quint exclaimed, "Damn it, I already told you how that was, Cole! I couldn't enforce no deadline while I had my hands full with this other business. I figured you'd think that was a hell of a lot more important, under the circumstances. Didn't give me no choice but to let the 3W stuff go through without raising a fuss over it."

"All right," Dorsey said, after a moment. "I'm not blaming you. But they *have* de-fied the deadline and now if we let it happen a second time we might as well forget the whole matter. Hatchet will be left a laughing stock!"

"What do you want done, then?" Quint demanded sullenly, while Nels McPhee switched his stare back and forth from one boss to the other, drinking it all in.

"Do you have to ask?" Cole Dorsey retorted. "Thanks to Olland, we've got a chance to undo some of the damage. Tomorrow, we've got to make sure those Ingrams have a surprise waiting for them."

"And old man Hardman? And the saddle tramp? What about them?"

"That'll be taken care of," Dorsey snapped. "*Everything* will be taken care of. But tomorrow morning it's the Ingrams! I want you to see they're taught a lesson none of those two-bit friends of theirs will ever forget."

Chapter 8

Bannister's instinct, the instinct of any hunted creature, was to climb, and he followed it more or less blindly. Since the valley proper was totally unfamiliar country, staying there would give his pursurers all the advantage. His best chance lay in getting above them and, with the settling night to help, losing them in that same rough up-and-down terrain where he'd been unable to elude them by daylight.

It wasn't going to be easy.

He had seen quite a lot of these hills today, but that was no help in trying to pick a way through them in pitch darkness. He could only trust to the sure-footedness of the chestnut, and to an outdoorsman's instinct to keep from becoming totally lost. He knew the ever-present risk of a bad stumble, or even a fall into an unseen precipice that could kill or cripple them both. Still, he had to keep on the move, as long as he didn't know what those Hatchet riders were up to.

There had been no further sight of them, before the last light of dusk faded out but once he heard a voice shouting somewhere behind him. The shout was swallowed up in the storm and wasn't repeated, though he halted the horse and strained to listen. Now, half an hour later, the rain slackened and presently ceased, but even so the night was filled with sound, the dripping from moisture-laden branches, the tearing of the wind through trees and brush. His enemies could be on his heels and he wouldn't know it.

Overhead, the clouds were beginning to break up and let some starlight through, to glimmer faintly on wet rocks and tree trunks. There would be no moon. He kept hunting for any landmark he might remember from riding through here earlier, but nothing he saw looked familiar.

The rising wind added to his troubles, because it carried the cold breath of the peaks and it cut like a knife through his drenched clothing. Bannister unstrapped Tacker's blankets and wrapped them about him as he rode, and this helped. He hunched in the saddle, chilled and aching from being dragged behind a galloping horse, and from the other punishment he'd taken.

The way got tougher. He lost all sense of time, and had no idea how deep it was into the night when he suddenly jarred himself erect to realize he'd dozed off in the saddle. With no one pushing it, the chestnut had come to a halt and was standing motionless under him, shifting position only to move about, hunting grass. Alarm shook Bannister and he drew his gun by reflex, head lifting and turning for any sound of danger.

He couldn't locate any. They had drifted into a bay of rock and timber where the wind was deflected, leaving an unnatural stillness. It was as sheltered a spot as he was apt to find. Bannister came to a sudden decision, there was nothing to be gained in driving himself and the horse to the point of exhaustion. He put the gun away, and dismounted. He staked the horse out on the rope he had found on its saddle; there was some coarse feed for it here, and puddles of rain water left from the storm. Where a couple of slabs of rock had tumbled together he found a comparatively dry niche for his own bed. He didn't risk a fire, and there was nothing to eat. Bannister wrapped himself in Tacker's blankets, and made himself as comfortable as he could against the raw chill.

He slept fitfully.

The first streaking gray of dawn brought him to his feet again, stiff and grimacing at the residue of pain left from the mistreatment of the day before. He stumped about, stretching cramped muscles, and tried to get his bearings.

Yesterday's storm was completely blown away; mist lay like thick cotton rope among the peaks where the snows still clung, and danced in streamers from rain-soaked rock and scrub. As the eastern sky began to take on a first flush of color, Bannister climbed until he could look over a wide stretch of timber and granite, falling away toward the valley below. During a long five minutes he could see no movement of any kind, and no lift of curling smoke that might have been from a campfire. He watched the fire of sunrise replace the remaining shadows of night, struck by the beauty of it and reasonably satisfied that none of the Hatchet riders would still be on his trail.

They could not have wanted him all that badly. Once they lost him in the night and the storm, they must have given up and turned back to report to headquarters.

As the day awakened, and the sun lifted to burn off the wavering mists from granite scarps, Bannister took a fresh look at the situation he now found himself in. He still could make little sense of it. All he definitely knew was that the storm center was the man named Hardman, hated by his neighbors, and at the same time obviously a victim of treachery from his own crew. And Jim Bannister was the only man in the world who knew just where Hardman was and how badly he was hurt.

His face was bleak as he turned back to where he had left the chestnut, gathered in the picket rope and rolled his borrowed blankets and tightened the cinch. After all this lapse of time, Nat Hardman could very well be dead; but if he should be alive, his only hope lay squarely with another hunted man. Under the circumstances, Jim Bannister couldn't abandon him.

He lifted into the saddle. By checking such landmarks as he was able, and the larger peaks across the valley of Colton Creek, he believed he had oriented himself. He knew roughly how far he must be from Hardman's cave. It remained to be seen if he could find it again, without stumbling into still more trouble, maybe more than he could handle.

A hundred yards below the hole in the rimrock, he pulled up in cover and waited for long minutes, checking the utter stillness. He was looking for any sign that the place had been discovered since he left it, or that he might have picked up an enemy who was trailing him now. It seemed unlikely, but a man who had been on the scout as long as Jim Bannister had learned not to trust appearances. Nat Hardman had already lain, wounded, in that hole for two nights; a few minutes more could hardly matter, and he had to be sure.

The sun shone warmly now; his clothing had finally dried on his body and the deep chill had gone, and with it, the worst of the soreness. He could still feel where Sid Tacker had slammed him in the kidney, but he probably looked worse than he felt — bedraggled, muddy, stubble-bearded and with a raw scab on one scraped cheek. Just like the range tramp people here had labeled him.

Impatience finally convinced him he was safe to move. He spoke to the horse, gave it a nudge with the spur and sent it up the final stretch. As he drew closer to the hole in the rock he peered and listened but could detect no sign of life within. He stepped down, anchored the reins to a bush, and entered.

At first look, he was sure it was a dead man who lay in front of him. He had seen enough of them in his time, and there was nothing in Hardman's limp sprawl to indicate any trace of life remained in him. But when he bent down beside the man and put a hand against his face, Bannister gave a grunt of surprise and almost jerked his hand away at the burning fever in Hardman's dry skin. Looking closer, then, he saw the rise and fall of his breathing.

The food and the panful of water left for the wounded man had been consumed, he noticed; apparently Hardman had rallied strength enough, at some time during these last hours, to drink and feed himself. Bannister settled back on his heels, rubbing his own beard-shagged cheeks as he studied the problem.

The presence of fever was a bad development. He took up the pan and went outside again.

He moved Sid Tacker's chestnut into the hollow where his own dun, well rested now, lifted its head in greeting. He got his saddle-bags, refilled the pan with spring water and went back into the cave. There, he managed to get some of the water between the hurt man's lips and then, carefully rolling him over onto his stomach, used a clean neckcloth to bathe the inflamed mouth of the bullet wound. It had not bled anymore, that he could tell. The cold water should help some against the fever, but what really mattered was getting that bullet out of there.

He had his clasp knife in his pack, but the point was nowhere near fine enough for such a task, and the very thought of attempting it himself was enough to make him cringe. No, there was only one choice. And that was really no choice at all.

Working furiously, he broke out his dwindling supplies and brewed coffee and mixed a batch of biscuits. The aroma of cooking seemed to reach Hardman for he stirred and his eyes opened. Bannister lifted him and got him to swallow some of the coffee, but when he tried to talk to the man Hardman's stare remained vacant and unseeing. "I need to get a doctor for you," Bannister insisted, speaking slowly and distinctly. "Can you tell me if there's one in the valley?"

He might have been talking to a stone. Hardman's stare wandered blankly over his face, and on to the low ceiling. His lips moved. Bending close, Bannister thought he heard a name. *"Sarah . . ."* And then something that sounded like, *"Cole . . . don't trust!"*

He was off again. Bannister swore, and let him down carefully.

It was no longer possible to avoid the alternatives. Either let this man die, or find him a doctor. It was a dilemma he had hoped not to have to face; he certainly had no business blundering down there, with all Hatchet hunting him. He didn't even know how or where to find the town. Pondering, he found himself rubbing at his jaw again, with a sigh he dropped his hand.

He might as well let well enough alone. So far, being taken for a range tramp had turned out to be a useful disguise. No one yet seemed to know who he was — a man with a fortune in syndicate bounty money riding on him. He decided to pass up, for now, the luxury of shaving. It would only use up valuable time. He had to be on his way.

He thought briefly of somehow trying to take Hardman with him, but he had to give that up at once. The man would never survive it; this country was too rugged even for an Indian travois. No, Hardman had to stay where he was. If there was help, the help would have to be brought to him.

Bannister set about making hasty preparations; more water, and coffee and biscuits, placed handy for the hurt man in case he should rally again, the chestnut to be unsaddled and picketed for future use.

Finally, with his gear and saddle strapped onto the dun, and a final check on the hurt man, he went out and swung astride.

If he had this to do, the quickest and most direct route was the best one, besides being the only one he knew. He had ridden it yesterday in the rain, surrounded by the Hatchet riders. Today, the sun was high and color had come back into the world, with light striking and splintering on pine branches and the shimmering quartz crystals of granite faces. The dun was rested and ready for travel. He eased down through the break in the fault scarp, where he had tolled Hatchet onto a false trail, and pushing steadily soon came to the place where he had been saved from a dragging by the unexpected appearance of Mort Woods and the Ingrams.

Vivid memory of that made him cautious, but there was no sign of danger now. He moved into the open, picked up the marks of cattle churned into the drying mud and followed them across the meadow's lower end where the drive trail from the valley entered. Knowing he was not apt to find a better route to the valley floor, Bannister put the dun into it.

It was, obviously, the way regularly taken

by cattle being moved to and from the upper reaches of hill graze; in time they had beaten out a wide and easy track, that picked its way over carefully chosen grades and switchbacks. At intervals its twists and turnings gave him brief glimpses of lower benches furred with timber, and of the valley floor itself. And almost at once he learned he was not the first to travel it today.

Two other riders had preceded him, within the past hour perhaps, and going in the same direction; this bothered him considerably. Any man he came across, Hatchet or not, could be a potential enemy. Riding in the wake of that unknown pair of horsemen, he found himself watching to make certain he kept them in front of him, and that he didn't allow their tracks to veer off unnoticed into the thickets of pines and brush that screened the edges of the trail, giving unlimited places for laying an ambush.

Thus, alert to danger as he was, Bannister was not caught by surprise when the first sharp spatter of gunfire broke out, somewhere farther down the marching, timbered ridges.

Besides themselves, the Ingram brothers' regular crew consisted of just one man —

Willie Ryker, an old puncher of long experience who admitted to sixty years but was both tough enough, and gnarled enough, that he might have been almost any age within twenty years on either side of that figure. Though nothing had ever been said about it, he was more a kind of partner than a mere hired hand. He and Bob and Farley batched it together in a one-room, board-and-batten shack. They shared the risks and the chores of the ranch equally, including the cooking. Since all the profits went back into the operation, save for the bare essentials of eating and smoking money and a new work shirt or pair of denims when absolutely necessary, it would have been very hard to tell who was working for whom.

Nor did Willie hesitate to tell the younger men off when he found them doing something counter to his better judgment and greater experience. And when he did they generally listened.

This morning he was in a sour and grumbling mood, but young Bob paid him no mind. Bob was feeling too good to let himself be bothered by an old man's predictions of trouble ahead, "I don't care how many times you tell me you made Russ Quint back down, yesterday! He ain't gonna *stay* backed down, nor is Cole Dorsey, or Hardman either. I got a bad feeling about it. If we run their deadline, I think we're gonna be sorry!"

"Nothing happened yesterday!" Bob reminded him.

"This ain't yesterday!" But, seeing that he was making no impression, the old fellow shrugged and let it go, keeping his grumblings to himself as they went out to rope and saddle their horses.

Willie Ryker and the ewe-necked old brown gelding that was his favorite work horse had an understanding, and there was never any cutting up when it came to making ready for the day's chores. Bob's sorrel, though, was cold-jawed and high-spirited on a morning as crisp as this one. It didn't want to take the bit, and once Bob was in the saddle it had to run him around the corral a time or two, nearly unseating him before he got the bucks ironed out of it. Bob liked a tussle and he was whistling and eager as they rode out through first light, to the meadow where their stock was bunched and ready for the day's drive.

A couple hundred head, of all ages, didn't make much of a herd, but after all, a ranching operation, in this high Colorado country, was limited by the amount of its winter range. It was the deep and protected valley that made stock growing possible at all, when most of the available graze lay along the steep spine of the Rockies. A Colton Creek rancher existed by feeding hay in winter, on the limited acreage of the valley bottom, and counting on getting his stock onto the summer meadows at the earliest moment receding snows permitted it. That was why any attempt to fence him off those meadows, with threats or with guns, could be disastrous if he failed to fight it.

And even if, on paper, a couple of hundred head might not look like much, they were plenty for two men to handle, especially when they didn't want to leave range that was familiar to them. Bob and Willie got them up and eased them into drifting over Colton Creek, letting them drink there; gradually they got the whole bunch moving. There was one five-year-old steer they kept around because he was a natural leader and, by now, knew the route to the high meadows as well as the men. He fell into his natural place at the front and after that with the riders swinging ropes and their trained cow-horses working to head up the animals that tried to turn back, the drive gradually began to shape up.

By then the sun had risen and the morning was starting to turn warm; the world looked green and new, after the rain. Bob Ingram was sweating and hoarse from yelling and swearing at the cattle; Willie Ryker was as scowlingly unruffled as ever. But the herd was moving well enough, and now they were climbing the first switchbacks of the broad drive trail and the valley flats were giving way to broken gullies and slab rock and the beginnings of timber. And that meant harder work, because it meant dodging through the yellow trunks and maneuvering the rough footing in time to intercept bunch quitters who wanted to try and lose themselves in the scrub.

Climbing this sheer west wall, that flung itself abruptly toward the sky, it didn't take long to gain altitude. When an hour crawled by, they were already well into the hills and drawing nearer the deadline. That was a place where the trail flanked a couple of upthrusts called the Pinnacles, and debouched into the lowest of the open meadows; it was here, according to report, that Hatchet had drawn the line. *Pass the Pinnacles, and you're in trouble.* Yesterday they had approached with rifles and nerves on end, and nothing at all had happened.

But that, as Willie Ryker pointed out, was yesterday.

More tense than he was willing to admit, Bob Ingram tried not to let himself think ahead. Just now, riding near the point of the slowly plodding column, he was watching an aspen growth that partly screened the broad trail, all too conscious of the way the lowing of the cattle covered possible sounds of danger. When a pair of horsemen broke into sight, half hidden for a moment by the flickering branches, he sucked in his breath and was quickly groping for the rifle in his saddleboot; the sorrel started to rear, feeling his startled drag on the reins. But the next moment he got it settled, and with a whoop of delight rammed the spurs and raced recklessly forward to meet his brother and Mort Woods.

Farley Ingram's sober face showed relief at seeing his younger brother in good shape and good spirits. He looked past Bob, at the cattle moving up toward them through scattered timber. He said, "You and Willie seem to be managing all right."

"It's kind of a job, for two men," Bob said, grinning and wiping a sleeve across his sweaty cheeks. "But we're making it."

"We figured you could use a couple of

extra hands. Mort's got his own beef pretty well settled, and no trouble yet. So we left his boys in charge, and dropped down to try and hurry things here a little."

"You checked the Pinnacles?" Bob asked anxiously. "Any sign of Hatchet?"

His brother shook his head. "Rode right past them. Couldn't see where anybody at all had been around."

"Then I guess it adds up, don't it?" The boy's grin flashed across his face. "Either there never was a deadline or we gave 'em second thoughts."

"Maybe." Mort Woods didn't sound convinced. "I'll feel better when we're safe into the hills with this herd. Let's get them moving."

With a couple of extra riders, it was not too much of a job to control the cattle, keep the stragglers up and the whole drive in shape and moving behind the leaders. They began to make some time, now; like a snake made of flowing red hides and glinting with sunlight on polished horns, the herd strung out along the climbing trail, the men flanking it and taking turns pushing the drag. And so at last they found themselves approaching the deadline; and without admitting it each man found himself tensing it up a little.

The muddy trail broke out of some timber and made a wide, climbing curve against the base of a stony ridge studded with boulders and scrub growth. Further ridges mounted behind this and, a little to the north, the peaks of the twin spires that were called the Pinnacles reared, their heads barely visible. In another half hour the herd should reach them. Farley Ingram, riding on the forward flank of the herd with Willie Ryker some thirty yards ahead of him, guessed that the old puncher was as nervous as he was. It showed in the way he kept swiveling his head to scan the surround, though they were still a distance below the supposed deadline.

Suddenly, in the rocks above them, Ingram caught a stabbing wink of light that he interpreted belatedly as the reflection of sunlight on metal. His reaction was a jerk at the rein that made the horse fling up its head; at the same moment he knew that Willie, too, must have seen the bright flash, but the older man reacted differently. With surprising quickness, he had the rifle out of his saddle scabbard and lifted to his shoulder, and now he fired in the direction on the ridge.

It might have been a signal. A spurt of smoke appeared, followed an instant later by the crack of an answering rifle. Immediately, behind screening boulders and trees and down logs all along the slope, hidden guns had opened a general barrage.

Appalled, frozen, Farley Ingram saw cattle being knocked off their feet and dropped, kicking. At once there was a bawling frenzy as unhurt animals, terrified by gunfire and the quick, hot smell of blood, frantically turned tail.

Willie Ryker was shooting back, standing in the stirrups to fire and lever and fire again. For his part, Farley Ingram seemed paralyzed for the moment; he forgot entirely about the rifle on his own saddle. He was jarred to his senses when he saw a bullet kick up dirt, a bare few yards away from him. In the next instant, horror gripped him as Willie suddenly reeled in the saddle and the rifle went spinning out of his hands, end for end.

Realizing his friend was hit, Ingram felt his throat distend on a shout that even he couldn't hear above the racket of gunfire and bawling cattle, and the pound of hoofs as the herd broke around him. A steer narrowly missed colliding with his horse and piling them up on the muddy, hoof-chopped ground. He kept a steady hand on the reins and settled his animal.

And then he was spurring forward to get to Willie, afraid that the old fellow was about to spill out of the saddle.

Reaching him, Ingram saw that an arm of the old Puncher's jacket had turned red with blood and that he had clamped a grip on the horn with his other fist to hold himself erect. The look he threw at the younger man was bitter and filled with pain, but he was swearing too fervidly to have been really bad hurt. "Hold on!" Ingram shouted above the other racket, and grabbed up the reins. As he did, a bullet sang past so close he thought he felt the tap of displaced air. Then he had both animals turned and was spurring for the shelter of the lower timber, towing Willie's mount behind him.

He glanced back anxiously once, saw that Willie was managing to keep his seat. Then the branches closed over their heads and bullets followed them in. When tree trunks surrounded them, Ingram pulled in and stepped down on legs that trembled. He got to Willie Ryker and laid an anxious hand on his knee as he peered again at the sleeve that was soaked with his friend's blood. "Willie!" he exclaimed. "How bad do you think it is?"

The wrinkled face was ashen with bullet

shock, but the old puncher managed a scornful answer. "Oh, hell! I'm all right. Takes more than a scratch like this to . . ." His eyes rolled up into his head and he sagged sideward.

Ingram moved quickly to catch him and ease his tough, wiry body to the ground. On his knees, he ripped away the bloody jacket sleeve to bare the wound in Ryker's upper arm. A bullet had sliced across the muscle but not too deeply; the bone wasn't harmed, and though it had bled a lot in the first minute it now seemed to have almost stopped. Farley shook with relief.

He lifted his head and peered about him, only now aware that the barrage of rifle fire from the ridge had slacked off, with no more than an occasional shot sending its echoes across the rock faces as a reminder that the enemy was still there. A last straggling steer came crashing though the underbrush and was gone, downslope. Now there was stillness, all the greater for the confusion and racket that had preceded it.

Farley Ingram rubbed a hand across his face, finding it wet with sweat; he looked out through the trees to where he could see a half dozen lifeless forms of cattle, lying where the fire from the ridge had dropped them. Otherwise, the Ingram herd had melted away and completely scattered. He let out trapped air from his lungs, and in the same moment heard his brother's voice calling anxiously somewhere below him.

He answered. "Here, Bob!" Moments later Bob came riding up through the scattered trees. He had a six-gun in his fist, and shock and anger stamped across his face. He pulled rein to stare at the old man lying motionless on the ground.

"Willie!" he cried. "Is he . . . ?"

Farley got to his feet. "It's not as bad as it looks," he said gruffly. "He'll be all right. Where's Mort?"

"I dunno," the kid said vaguely. "Back yonder somewhere." He wet his lips as he looked at his brother. "I heard the shooting, and I knew you and Willie was up front. I thought they'd likely got you both!"

"No, but they sure busted up this drive!" Farley Ingram, who almost never swore, let go with a few choice ones. He added, shaking his head, "I was dead wrong! There sure enough was a deadline, all right, and somehow they found out we were figuring to cross it. But how? How they could know, that's what I can't figure out! Because, they were all set up and waiting for us." Suddenly a bad thought struck him, and he stepped closer and caught at his brother's arm. "Bob! *You* didn't talk to anyone, did you? You or Willie didn't happen to mention to anybody what we were planning?"

He saw the terrible look that came into his brother's face. Bob said hotly, "Damn you! How could you think a thing like that?"

"Bob, I only —" And then he broke off, because, mingled with the quick anger, he thought he read something else on the younger man's anguished face: bitterness, and guilt and shame. Bob blinked his eyes, almost as though fighting back a scald of tears.

Abruptly he kicked the horse with the spur, wrenching his arm from Farley's grasp. In horror, Farley watched him spurring through the trees into the open, headed directly for the slope where the slaughtered cattle lay stiffening, as though he meant to charge the rifles entrenched on the side of the ridge. "Come back!" Farley Ingram shouted. "You trying to get yourself killed? *Bob!*"

He doubted his brother even heard him.

Chapter 9

From the sound of gunfire, Bannister had to believe someone meant business. After a first tentative pair of shots, like adversaries feeling one another out, the noise quickly built and was redoubled by its own echoes, until he couldn't tell if there were only a few guns or many. He had halted to listen, reluctant to get any closer or find himself caught up in any more of other people's quarrels. But being under pressure himself, he decided at last, that he was going to have to investigate. If his route was blocked, he would simply have to find some way to go around.

So he rode warily ahead. The trail dropped him down another turn through the trees, and then abruptly the timber opened, and the land fell away and it was almost as though a vantage point had been arranged for him.

It looked as though someone must have blundered into a trap. He thought there might be a half dozen rifles ensconced in the rocks just below him. Hard to count them exactly, for the firing was confused, and spurts of muzzle smoke melted together in the wind that raked the slope. But it was easy enough to see the damage they'd done, in the motionless shapes of dead animals lying along the foot of the ridge. Even as he looked, the bulk of the herd was scattering, bawling with terror, back into the lower trees. Though they had no targets left, the rifles continued pouring out their fire. Finally they slacked off and an uneasy quiet settled. On the flat, nothing moved.

By now Bannister had his glasses and was studying the torn-up ground, but he didn't seem to locate any bodies of men among the slaughtered beef. Whoever that herd belonged to must have made it to cover. So he shortened the focus of his lenses and looked for the ambushers on the slope just below him. Due to the broken ground he could not locate them all, but he picked out a couple, brought so close that it seemed he might almost have reached down and touched them. All he could see of them, though, were their hunched shoulders and the wide brims of their hats, not enough to tell him anything about them.

It didn't matter, since this hardly looked

133

like any of his business. During the past twenty-four hours he had seen quite enough of the tangled affairs and complex hatreds of this range, and he was already in as deep as he could afford to get. Whatever he was witnessing, it only concerned him by being in his way. Lowering the glasses he asked himself if he should wait where he was and see what happened, or try to find a detour that would get him past this unexpected roadblock.

And then a single rider was bursting out of those trees and charging straight at the slope. The riflemen had been wanting a target; at once they opened up. Undaunted, the horseman came in at a dead run, right into the teeth of the barrage. He had a pistol and he started shooting back at his enemies long before he was in short-gun range, a futile gesture anyway, from the back of a plunging horse. And now he hit steeper going that slowed his wild charge. His heels flailed his animal's sides; the sorrel's head bobbed to the effort of the climb. But there was no hint of turning back, though with his enemies concentrating all their fire on him it seemed only a matter of seconds before they would bring him down.

Jim Bannister swore. He was already incensed enough over the careless destruction; now it suddenly seemed wrong to stand and watch a game sacrifice made against such odds. Forgetting his determination not to get involved, he was sliding the rifle from its boot as he dropped to the ground. A few running strides took him at an angle down the slope, to bring up behind a rock outcrop. Here, he had excellent position. He snapped the saddle gun to his shoulder and started shooting.

It seemed to take the riflemen a moment to realize somebody had high gun on them. Jim Bannister knocked the hat off the head of one and sent it skimming across the empty air; he ducked and whirled and Bannister caught a glimpse of his face. In a way it was not too surprising that he remembered having seen the man yesterday evening, in the living room at Hatchet. An ambush like this seemed, somehow, very much Coleman Dorsey's style of warfare.

The next bullet struck a bolder and sprayed up a glittering cloud of rock chips around the one who had been using it as a rest for his saddle gun. It sent the man reeling back, dropping his weapon and frantically clutching at his face with both hands. Bannister continued firing, as rapidly as he could work the lever, and belatedly now the

Hatchet crew became aware that something had gone wrong. All at once they seemed to forget the rider below them, they were too concerned with the threat from this new angle. They turned their guns on Bannister but he was too well positioned; there really was no way they could hope to get at him. One did manage to put a bullet uncomfortably close. He didn't flinch, but coldly continued to work the trigger and a moment later knocked over the man who had fired it.

He was angry, but he hadn't actually been aiming to kill; it sobered him. With the next shot he was careful to pull low and hit the ground in front of his target, showering him with grit. That was enough, though. Not trying for his shot, the man suddenly started running. Next moment they had all caught the contagion of panic and were going away from there as quickly as they could; the one who had been blinded by rock chips stumbled and fell, scrambled up again, still pawing at his face.

At the same time, the rider who had charged the slope, singlehanded, made the top of it with his sorrel laboring between his knees. His face, young and clean-shaven, was flushed with anger and excitement as he yelled and brandished an empty six-shooter. Bannister gave him only a glance, being more interested just then in the Hatchet riflemen. A bulge of rock and scrub had just put them out of his range of vision. Leaving his place he started across the steep face of the ridge, fighting loose rubble.

When he got to a point where he could pick them up again they were out of easy rifle shot and he lowered the smoking weapon, holding the hot tube in his hands as he watched the five fleeing men weave their way through the hillside growth and disappear into a stand of scrub pine. They had horses there; he heard them breaking into motion, hoofbeats swelling briefly and then fading as loose footing sopped up the noise.

He stood a moment, still listening, feeling let down in this aftermath of the fight.

He supposed the Hatchet crew had accomplished what they set out to, by turning back those cattle on the drive trail; no reason, then, for them to stay and brave the rifle that had got in above them. So he had no particular feeling of scoring a victory. Instead, the thought of the one he had shot returned now, and it weighed heavily. Jim Bannister had never reached the point of taking killing for granted.

He turned and walked toward the place where his victim lay sprawled across the shining tube of his rifle, face turned to the sky. The rider from below had dismounted, to stand holding the reins of the sorrel in one hand and his six-shooter in the other, staring blankly at the dead man. He lifted his head sharply as Bannister approached. "Who was he?" Bannister asked.

"I never heard his name," the young fellow said. "But I've seen him. He's one of them new hands Hatchet's been bringing in; they've had Russ Quint out scouring the landscape, looking for guns to hire."

Bannister nodded. He knew all about that. He himself had been mistaken, by Coleman Dorsey, for one of those hired gunfighters.

The stranger was still peering at him intently. Suddenly he said, "I know *you.* You're the range tramp Quint wanted to hang yesterday. Farley took you away from him."

That startled Bannister into a closer look. He had thought there was something vaguely familiar about the other, but now he saw a definite family resemblance. "And you must be the one that hung back and put a rifle on Quint, to help make him behave himself. Another Ingram, I guess. You two look alike."

"We're brothers. I'm Bob Ingram."

It was a development that, for some reason, had never occurred to him. Bannister said, "I never had a chance to thank either of you properly. Except for you, I'd probably have had my neck stretched."

"Is that the reason you bought in just now?"

He shook his head. "I had no idea who was involved. It just looked to me like an unfair fight. Besides, I never did enjoy to see good cattle being shot to pieces. I had an idea someone had been tolled into a trap. I just hope this didn't come out of what you did on my account."

"No connection at all," Bob Ingram assured him. "It was a matter of a deadline."

He might have explained further but now another horseman joined them, spurring his sweating horse up the steep ridge face. The newcomer was Farley Ingram, and he looked badly worked up. He didn't appear to notice Jim Bannister, or the dead man either. He reined in beside his brother and leaned to grab the younger man by a shoulder, and his voice shook as he exclaimed, "Damn it, that was the stupidest thing I ever seen you do, charging head-on up this hill! Were you trying to get yourself killed?"

Bannister caught the darkness in Bob Ingram's face as he squirmed free. "I'm still in one piece," he muttered. "This gent busted in on them, dropped one and sent the others running." And he indicated Jim Bannister.

"You?" The older brother looked at Bannister, and then at the limp shape on the ground. "So *that's* what happened. I couldn't figure, except all at once there seemed to be a hell of a lot of shooting." His voice turned heavy with bitterness. "Well, and why shouldn't they leave? They done what they was sent to." But he found it in him to add, "Anyway, I have to thank you. It looks like you saved the kid's hide for him."

"Then maybe we can say I evened our score a little," Bannister said gruffly.

After that, thinking the two brothers might have something to say that a stranger didn't need to overhear, he turned back up the loose hillside footing to where he had left his horse.

Shoving the rifle in the boot, he stood a moment holding the reins and listening to the stillness of the high country. Except for the ugly reminder of death, in the man he had killed and a dozen motionless shapes of cattle, it would be hard to believe what had been going on here a few short minutes ago.

He mounted, and rode back down to join the brothers, who were examining the body of the dead man. Meanwhile two more riders had come up from below. One of these was Mort Woods, the Ingrams' friend; the other was a weatherbeaten-looking cowpuncher with a blood-soaked sleeve. He was a tough one, though. He had obviously taken a bullet, but he rode straight up and only the fierce scowl on his wrinkled face indicated that he might be in pain.

As Bannister approached, Mort Woods squinted at him and suddenly the rancher cursed and brought up the gun from his holster. "By God!" he said loudly. "Didn't I make it clear, yesterday, if I saw you again I'd shoot you myself?"

But then Farley Ingram had stepped close enough to reach and grab the man's arm and pull it down. "Mort, you don't understand! We owe this man. He stepped in and busted up that whole bunch of Hatchet gunmen!"

Woods glowered at Bannister, his face

ugly with disbelief. But finally he shook off Ingram's hand and shoved his gun deep into the holster, and he said sourly, "I didn't see it, so I'll have to take your word for it. But seems to me I also took your word for it when you said Hatchet hadn't really set up any deadline, that we'd all been scaring ourselves with rumors! And you see the result!" The wave of his hand was eloquent enough. "I dunno how we got my herd through, yesterday, unless they just had their hands too full to bother with us. But this one's scattered to hell and gone and Willie Ryker's been shot and what further bright ideas do you have?"

Farley Ingram had gone red in the face under his bitter sarcasm, but Ingram was plainly a placid-tempered man who did not rouse to anger easily. He kept a rein on his tongue now as he answered, patiently, "It looks like I was wrong, sure enough. I guess I was just too hopeful, too anxious to grab at any sign we were mistaken, about Hardman and Cole Dorsey wanting to fight the Valley. I take the blame. As to what happens next, I admit I just don't know. My brain is still numb!"

Woods seemed only a little appeased by the way the other took his tongue-lashing. He shrugged and said, "Well, I guess I know what I have to do! That herd of mine looks like the next target. I got to get back up there and be ready to give my riders a hand, and I better not waste time about it!"

He was already kicking his horse into motion, with a last suspicious stare for Jim Bannister, as he pulled away and started at an angle across the slope. Farley Ingram called after him, "Hadn't you better wait for us, Mort? You may need help."

"We'll manage," the other answered shortly, over a shoulder. "So far, you've been a jinx. Worry about your own herd. You got a couple of hundred head of beef losing themselves in the hills!"

And then he was gone; and Willie Ryker cursed with disgust and the pain of his furrowed arm. "If *that's* how he feels about it."

"Well, maybe from his point of view he's right." Farley Ingram sounded discouraged, suddenly borne down by weariness. He rubbed a hand across his face. "I ain't done too good. Yesterday I got him involved in a near shootout with Russ Quint; and I was the one made the mistake about Nat Hardman's deadline."

With Woods gone, the silence had returned to the hillside. The horses stomped and stirred restlessly. The man on the ground seemed to grow deader by the minute. Bannister drew a breath. He suddenly felt he had to speak. He said slowly, "This Nat Hardman, did it ever occur to you, you could be making a mistake about him?"

Frowning, Farley Ingram demanded, "What do you mean? What kind of mistake?"

"I don't really know how to begin. But, you all seem convinced that Hardman's the root of your trouble. And just what makes you so sure?"

Willie Ryker scowled as he nursed his hurt arm. "Hell, I guess we ought to know who we're fighting!"

"You've seen the kind of crew he hires," Farley Ingram pointed out. "Here lies one that you were forced to kill, yourself. Doesn't that answer your question?"

"But the crew was hired by a man named Coleman Dorsey."

"Who is Nat Hardman's son-in-law," Ingram replied. "Practically his partner. Those two are hand in glove." And Willie Ryker said amen to that: "They're a real pair, all right!"

Bannister hesitated, knowing he might be about to make a dreadful mistake; still, he and he alone held the key that could make sense of this situation. It seemed an effort had to be made. "What if I could prove for a fact," he said, "that you're wrong? What if I told you that Nat Hardman was shot at Dorsey's orders, by a member of his own crew, a man named Tacker. And that I know where he's lying hurt, with the bullet in him while Dorsey has every rider he can spare out trying to find him and finish him off?"

They all three stared at him. Finally Farley Ingram said, with a slow shake of the head, "Hardman and Dorsey are fighting? That would be awfully damned hard to believe. For one thing, even if Hardman might have been shot, what makes you think it was Sid Tacker's doing?"

"I heard Tacker brag about it! Let's go back to the beginning," Bannister persisted earnestly. "Yesterday I rode into this country, a complete stranger, not knowing anybody at all. Entirely by accident I came across Nat Hardman, where he'd crawled off to hide from Quint and the others." He gave a description of the hurt man, and saw in his hearers' faces that they recognized it beyond any doubt. "I had no idea what the thing was all about," Bannister went on, "but I couldn't see letting a man be murdered as he lay helpless; so I took his horse and used it to try to draw his enemies off the trail. They caught up with me and were trying to force me to tell where I'd left him. That's when you stepped in and made them turn me loose." He added, "That's what I was doing, riding Nat Hardman's horse."

He let the story sink in, waiting for their reaction and their questions. It was Farley Ingram who asked the one he dreaded. His head shot forward, his troubled stare pinned on the stranger's face, he demanded harshly: "*Who are you?* I can't believe you're any ordinary, dollar-a-gross range drifter!"

Bannister met his look as he gave the answer he had ready. "Let's just say I'm someone that's been chased, shot at, pistol-whipped, and dragged and had a hangnoose around his neck — and none of that inclines me to be friendly to Coleman Dorsey or Russ Quint or anyone connected with them. What's more I happen to believe you've got some dead-wrong notions about a man you call your enemy, when, as a matter of fact, it seems clear to me you both belong on the same side."

"That don't necessarily follow," Willie

Ryker said harshly. "Even if Hardman and Dorsey might have had a falling out, one's just as big a bastard as the other! I've known Hardman for years and believe me, the name fits him!"

"Maybe you're right," Bannister admitted. "But think of this a moment, right now he's hurt, and helpless, with every man's hand against him and his own crew trying to find him in order to finish him off. But if you were to join forces and win it could change the whole complexion of things between Hatchet and its neighbors."

"I see what you mean," Ingram said, but there was a note of heavy doubt in his voice. "Still, before I can believe this, I've got to see proof with my own eyes. That herd of ours is scattered so bad now, it can wait awhile. How about it? Will you take us where the old man's hiding?"

"Only if I have your word that you'll do nothing to harm him. I wouldn't deliver any man over to his enemies."

The other nodded. "And I don't believe in kicking any man when he's down, and can't help himself. So you've got my word. Who knows, maybe Hardman's in a position, now, when he at least might have to listen to reason!"

"If he can still hear anything," Bannister

147

reminded him. "He's in desperate straits — it was sometime evening before last that he was shot. It's a wonder to me he's lasted this long. But if there's a chance it will do any good I'll take you to him."

They left the dead man where he lay. As Willie Ryker said sourly, "He's Hatchet's responsibility. If they want him, let them come back and get him!" Jim Bannister couldn't be that callous about it, but they had no way to dig a grave and he had an urgent feeling that time could not be wasted. Now that the decision was made, he waited impatiently for the Ingrams to take to their saddles. Ryker had never dismounted, probably because with his hurt arm it was less painful to stay where he was.

Bannister noticed that Bob Ingram had had virtually nothing to say during all the talk, the young fellow seemed withdrawn, as though working over dark problems of his own. His older brother, too, must have been bothered by this, for now he stopped Bob as the latter was turning his horse and Bannister heard Farley say, "I'm sorry I bawled you out, kid. Especially what I said about you talking too much, spilling to somebody what we meant to do this morning. I should know you got better sense than that! I can't blame you for getting mad at me, and maybe letting that push you into taking foolish chances. Forgive me?"

Bob gave his brother no more than a single anguished glance, and then he ducked his head and broke away without a word. Bannister frowned. That young man was carrying some kind of a heavy burden, much greater than his brother probably had any suspicion.

But, having made his apology, Farley seemed to think the matter was settled. He lifted into the saddle and looked at Bannister. "You haven't told me what to call you."

He seemed to miss the stranger's brief hesitation. "Jim will do."

"All right then, Jim. I guess we're ready. Lead out."

Bannister lifted the reins. He voiced a solemn warning. "Ride easy! The last thing we want is for Hatchet to see us, and guess where I'm taking you."

The other nodded understanding. "Don't worry," he said. "I'll bring up the rear. And believe me, I'll be using the eyes in the back of my head!"

Chapter 10

Even with his decision made, Bannister wasn't quite able to shake the nagging thought that he could be making a mistake and betraying Nat Hardman, by revealing his hiding place. But the secret he carried had been growing more burdensome with each hour that passed, as his personal danger grew. And something told him that Farley Ingram was a man of tractable instincts who would keep his word.

So he set a fast pace, though a careful one; they saw no other riders in the hills and when they approached the cave he was reasonably sure no one had followed them. Farley Ingram saw his hurried look around and told Bob to keep a watch. The other three dismounted and made the climb to the narrow opening in the rock.

This time, in Bannister's absence, the wounded man did not seem to have moved at all; the water and food were untouched. Bannister looked at Ingram and received the latter's grim, confirming nod. "I don't understand, but it looks like you told it straight. This is Hardman, sure as the devil."

"And he ain't in good shape!" Willie Ryker muttered. He went down on one knee, careful about that bullet-stiffened arm; he touched the check that was bright with fever, thumbed a lower lid and peered into the wounded man's eye, felt for a pulse. "He ain't good at all!"

The pulse was feeble, grown alarmingly so in the time since Bannister last checked it. Carefully he turned Hardman over and lifted the crude bandage, to show the hole where lead had entered his back. Farley Ingram sucked in his breath. He said, "That thing's got to come out of there! I doubt he can live long enough for a doctor to work on him."

"If I'd had a decent knife," Jim Bannister said in the hushed tones they were all using, as though afraid the injured man would hear them, "I might almost have tried to dig it out myself."

"Well, I got a knife," Willie Ryker said, and produced it from a sheath sewed in the side of his boot. "But I'd never have nerve enough to try anything like that!"

It looked like a good knife, with a bone handle and a narrow blade that gleamed in the dim light of the cave. Reluctantly, Bannister took it and felt the keen edge, the fine point. The three men looked at one another. Farley Ingram swallowed, hard. "What do you think? We can still send Bob down to fetch Doc Allen, and hope for the best."

"We'd never get him here in time!" said Willie, emphatically. "There ain't much left of this man. And if that thing stays where it is, he hasn't got a chance."

Bannister saw the same thought in Ingram's face, confirming his own. His hand tightened on the knife handle and he felt sweat break out of him. But he nodded grimly. "Somebody get a fire going," he said, "for better light and to heat this blade. Tell Bob to keep a good lookout. There's been an awful lot of travel to and from this cave, and by now the trail probably wouldn't be too hard for Hatchet to follow if they should once pick it up.

"I've never done anything like this before, but I've got a pretty steady hand, I'm willing to give it a try."

Ingram ran a tongue over lips that had gone dry. "All right. What can we do to help?"

"You'll have to hold him. Hold him good! If he makes the slightest move, I'll probably kill him."

When it came down to the moment, with Ingram and Ryker kneeling at either side of the wounded rancher and the knife heated and ready in his hand, Bannister wasn't sure he could go through with it. His revulsion was so strong that he shuddered and his whole arm shook. But he set his teeth, and somehow forced himself to insert the blade and begin his probe.

If Hardman had been conscious, he knew he could never have done this. It was almost as though he could feel the sharp point work its way blindly, by touch, deeper into torn and bloody muscle. Once Hardman moaned and stirred slightly, despite the hands that held him; sweat broke out on Bannister's forehead and he hastily let go of the knife's bone handle. When his helpers had renewed their hold on the unconscious man, he had to flex tense and aching fingers before he could bring himself to touch the thing again.

Long seconds later, the point scraped against something he knew could not be bone. He caught his breath as he tested the obstruction with careful movements. Farley Ingram, watching his face, read the tightening of his expression and asked quickly, "Found it?"

Bannister nodded. The slightest twist of

the blade got its point beneath the bullet and he cautiously increased pressure against this leverage; suddenly, without warning, the bullet was dislodged and popped free of the wound. Bannister withdrew the blood-soaked knife and his hands were trembling with reaction.

Willie Ryker quickly snatched up the bloody bit of lead. Holding it on his palm, he said in a voice edged with the strain they had all been under, "Ain't it hell, that a thing no bigger'n this can lay a strong man low?" To Bannister he added gruffly, "You go get yourself some air. We can do whatever else is needful."

"Thanks!"

He got outside, on legs that seemed for a moment unable to hold him up. He thought he was definitely going to be sick, but the air that struck coldly against his sweating face saved him. Nothing ever felt better. He stood dragging deep breaths into his lungs, and gradually the tremors in his muscles subsided.

Now Farley Ingram came to join him. Ingram was building a cigarette with fingers that were none too steady. When he saw Bannister's face he silently offered it to him; Bannister accepted the smoke with a nod of thanks, and the match that the other struck on a thumbnail to light it. Rolling another cigarette for himself while the tall man took deep drags at the first one, Ingram said, "Willie's taking care of him. The hole bled quite a bit, at first, and that's good because it lessens the risk of blood poisoning. You got a steady hand, all right, Jim. Thanks to you and your emergency surgery, the man may have a chance. But he still needs Doc Allen just as fast as we can get him up here!"

"I can do that, Farley." Bob Ingram had come climbing up to them. "I been looking close, but there's no sign at all of anyone on our trail. So why don't I ride down to town, and fetch the doc?"

Farley Ingram hesitated. "I was thinking that would be my job."

"No! I want to do it!" Bob insisted, almost too emphatically Bannister thought, and was again struck by an odd feeling of something gnawing at the young fellow. "Don't worry. I'll hunt him out, wherever he is, and I'll bring him if I have to tie him on his saddle!"

"What about this Allen?" Bannister asked quickly. "Can he be trusted?"

"He's reliable," Ingram assured him. "Besides, he's one of the few good friends Nat Hardman has in the Valley."

"But, the way things have stood between Hardman and the Ingrams, will it seem likely you'd go out of your way to get him help?"

That question hadn't occurred to Farley Ingram. Seeing him hesitate, frowning over it, his brother Bob said quickly, "Don't worry. I'll think of some yarn to get him up here."

Farley considered, and nodded. "All right, Bob. Just don't waste any time. And I guess I don't have to tell you to ride wary of Hatchet!"

Bob, close-mouthed and nursing whatever grievance was troubling him, didn't bother to answer that; he turned away, saying, "I'll fetch my bronc."

Jim Bannister let him get a half dozen steps away before he called after him, on a sudden decision, "Bring mine while you're at it."

Farley Ingram looked at Bannister. When Bob had gone out of earshot he asked. "You're riding, Jim? Yes, I think that's only right. You've already done more than anyone had a right to expect, seeing that it wasn't your fight. You've delivered Nat Hardman into safe hands; I've already given my word on that. Now I think you *should* leave before you get in deeper."

"But I'm not leaving. I've got a notion about this business," Bannister explained, as the other stared at him. "Remains to be seen if it's any good. But meanwhile, your brother can show me a quicker route down to the valley than I could find for myself."

"Well, of course. But I don't understand! Why should you want to go any further with this?"

"Hatchet's given me a couple of reasons," Bannister said grimly. "And then, another thing occurs to me. The important thing right now is get that doctor up here, and it looks as though your brother tends to be impulsive. If he should run into some kind of trouble, by being along I could maybe steer him away from it and make sure he does his errand."

Farley Ingram drew a breath. "You must be reading my mind. I'd never have let him go, if the kid hadn't been so insistent. I'll feel a hell of a lot easier if he has you along."

"Then that's settled."

They got some sharply suspicious looks from the youngster when Bob learned he was to have company, but he offered no argument. His brother was plainly full of questions about Bannister's reason for wanting to make the ride, but he wouldn't come out and ask and Bannister remained close-mouthed. The idea he had was actually so tenuous, being derived from a few broken words that had passed Nat Hardman's lips in the delirium of fever, that he had no intention of discussing it with anyone.

He took a last look at Hardman, thought the man seemed at least none the worse for the crude surgery he had undergone. Bannister left the cave and swung into the saddle, joining Bob Ingram who was already mounted and impatient to be gone. The older brother and the veteran puncher Willie Ryker, who would be remaining, watched solemnly as they rode away.

As Bannister had said, it made all the difference in the world whether a man was riding blind, or traveling with an experienced guide. Bob Ingram must know every mile of this country. He scarcely seemed to falter in picking a route. Stopping only to rest the horses, they worked their way steadily down from alpine meadows into spruce and fir, and then into the bench country where scattered yellow pine stood straight amid grassy parks that were almost free of underbrush.

Without immediate pressure, Jim Bannister was able to enjoy the beauty of treeheads wheeling against a deep sky, and the sparkle of flashing streams that spilled in rock-throated waterfalls. It was fine country, all right, the best kind of cattle country, though its use would always be restricted because of the limited amount of winter range in the narrow valley of Colton Creek.

Which perhaps made it inevitable, though none the less sad, that men would be fighting over it.

Piecing together what he had been able to learn about the conflict, mostly from the things Farley Ingram told him, he gathered that Nat Hardman had been first to come here and set up in the cattle business. At one time, apparently, he had controlled virtually the entire valley, holding onto it with a hardness of determination that had made other, envious men, keep their distance. It seemed to have been the sudden death of his wife that changed all that, blunting his ambitions with grief and making him indrawn and indifferent. In the years after that he had scarcely noticed or reacted when new brands began to filter in and take up room along Colton Creek and in the high summer pastures.

But now there seemed to have been another abrupt reversal; now Hatchet was moving out again, pushing against its neighbors, trying to take back range that Hardman had let slip from his grasp. And the difference, Bannister gathered, was Coleman Dorsey. It was Cole Dorsey who, having married into Hatchet, seemed determined to see it once again as powerful as it had been before. Whatever the moral right or wrong of that, Jim Bannister couldn't condone his way of going about it.

Not turning his gunmen loose to slaughter good beef crossing an illegal deadline, or to murder a man who trusted him, or, for that matter, to give a total stranger the kind of treatment they'd handed Jim Bannister.

Young Ingram maintained a brooding silence, and they talked very little. When at last they came down the creek itself, lined with poplar and willow and swollen with yesterday's rain, Bannister casually asked, "How do you get to Hatchet from here?"

That got him a sharp look. "Why, you just follow this creek road north through town," Bob said. "But, you surely ain't going anywhere near there again?"

"Just getting my bearings." Bannister let it go at that, and his companion fell again

160

into sullenness. The older man was still trying to imagine what could be eating at him. It must be something pretty serious.

The town showed ahead, its roofs visible among newly-leafed heads of cottonwood and alder. Approaching the wooden bridge at the main street's upper end, Bannister tried another question. "What happens if this doctor of yours isn't home?"

Bob Ingram seemed to drag himself out of his black mood long enough to consider. "Then I guess we look for him. The doc ain't married, he lives alone, and he's apt to take off without any warning and go fishing or something. But, maybe he'll have left word."

"Or maybe we'll be in luck."

The young fellow only shrugged, in a way that suggested he no longer believed much in luck or in anything else. And Bannister let it go, because now they had entered the town, a few drab houses lining a street where puddles from yesterday's rain shone in the sun.

As always, there was uneasiness, the sense of danger and of prying, hostile eyes, that came upon a fugitive when he deliberately let the buildings of some unknown settlement close about him. Bannister had to steel himself against this, his hand steady on the reins and his questing glance busily probing doors and windows. Slouching in the saddle in order to diminish his betraying size, he sensed that his best protection from curious stares lay in the shag of yellow beard stubble, and the clothing torn and muddied during his ordeal at the end of Sid Tacker's lass rope. The more that people continued to take him for an impoverished drifter or a harmless range tramp, the less likely they were to guess that he could have a fortune in syndicate bounty riding on his head.

Abruptly, his companion pulled rein and Bannister saw the tightness of the muscle that ridged his jaw. He quickly followed the direction of young Ingram's stare, but could see nothing more than a store building with the name, OLLAND'S MERCANTILE, painted on its false front, above the porch overhang. A girl was busy with a broom, sweeping her way through the wide double doorway. As she stepped out onto the porch, she lifted her head and discovered the pair of riders sitting motionless, watching her.

She was a small girl, not too pretty, rather thin, with pale yellow hair pulled back into a bun. She gave Bannister scarcely a glance; her stare fastened on young Ingram, and her lips parted but no words came from them. She leaned her broom against the side of the doorway, and hurried to the steps.

Now she found her voice. "Bob!" she cried. "Is everything all right? Are *you* all right?"

Bannister saw the corner of the young fellow's mouth work. Bob Ingram said, with bitter sarcasm, "Couldn't be better!"

A hand lifted to her throat as she stared at him. "What do you mean? What happened, Bob? Did something go wrong?"

"You should know!" he answered harshly, and now he jerked the rein and edged his sorrel over beside the porch. In that moment Bannister thought he understood everything, even before the young man cried hoarsely, "Margie, how could you do it? How *could* you? I thought we were friends! Maybe even a little more than that."

Her face drained of color. Shaking her head a little she stammered, "Do *what* Bob? I don't understand."

"They were all set for us!" he cried, and one hand reached and gripped her shoulder so hard Bannister saw her wince. "They *knew!* They were waiting, and they shot the herd to ribbons and scattered it and poor Willie Ryker took a bullet that might have killed him. We could *all* have been killed!"

"But you don't think *I* . . . ?" She couldn't finish.

"Will you tell me who else? You're the only one I told!" Bob's voice broke and suddenly Bannister suspected he was crying. "I lied to my brother, I said I didn't tell anyone, and yet it was my fault all along. I played the traitor because I thought you were someone I could trust!"

"Bob, I swear I never said a word! Not to anyone!" But in a frenzy of grief and shame and disappointment the boy had begun to shake her, blindly, until her head rocked upon her shoulders and her long fair hair came undone from its pins. Bannister stayed out of this, up to now, but suddenly he was afraid young Ingram would actually hurt the girl without really meaning to. Just as he was about to intervene, there was an interruption from another quarter.

A man, small and bespectacled and pale-haired like the girl, with enough resemblance that they must surely be closely related, had emerged from the store entrance. Now he let out an angry cry, and rushed forward to seize Margie by an arm and jerk her out of the young man's grasp. "Why, damn you, Bob Ingram!" he shouted, his high-pitched voice trembling and excited. "Take your hands off her!" He flung a protective arm around the girl, who had clapped her hands to her face and was weeping. Young Ingram, gaping blankly, had the dazed look of someone coming up from an immersion of cold water.

"I always knew you were no-good trash!" the man cried, making ineffective gestures with one clenched fist. "This only proves it! I should never have let you hang around any niece of mine. I wouldn't, had I realized how thick you two were getting! All the big talk and brag you were making in front of her yesterday about how tough you Ingrams are, and what-all you were going to do to Nat Hardman. . . ."

His words trailed off suddenly, as he looked at the change in the young man's face. Bob Ingram's head had lifted and he was staring at him with terrible eyes. "D'you mean it was you, Gil Olland? That's it, isn't it? You were listening to Margie and me and you went to Hatchet with what you heard!"

The storekeeper might have tried to deny it, but his face gave him away. His niece, pulling free of him, stared at him aghast and cried, out of a depth of hurt, "Uncle Gilbert! You *didn't!*" Gone red to the roots of his thinning pale hair, Gil Olland set his jaw stubbornly, his very silence an admission.

Carried by anger, Bob Ingram actually started down from his saddle, as though he meant to go after the merchant then and there. Seeing this, Olland's defiance was touched by fear and he dropped back a step. Jim Bannister decided matters were getting out of hand and he said sharply, "Bob! Not now! Remember what we're here for."

It seemed to sink home; young Ingram held where he was. But his voice shook with anger as he told the storekeeper, "If you weren't Margie's uncle, I ain't sure what I might do!" He looked at the girl, then, and in bitterness and shame he said, "All day I been blaming *you* for what happened! I don't see how you can ever forgive me."

She quickly shook her head and lifted a hand toward him. "No. It's all right Bob. I — I can see how it must have looked." But Bannister could tell that she had been terribly hurt. He felt suddenly sorry for both of them.

He told Bob, "I think we better ride."

The young fellow nodded glumly, and gave his horse a nudge with the spur. Bannister fell in beside him and they rode on, putting their backs to Olland's where the man and the girl stood watching them go.

Chapter 11

Jim Bannister told the young man, "You should feel better, now you know what really happened. You've been blaming yourself, and you've been blaming the girl. But you see now, you were neither of you at fault. You had no way of knowing her uncle was eavesdropping on you or that he'd carry tales to Hatchet."

The other's dark look didn't alter. He shrugged heavily. "That don't help much. It don't excuse what I said to her!"

"Oh, she won't hold that against you. She understands." But his arguments seemed to be having little effect and Bannister let it go. These young people would have to work out their own problems. Given time, they probably could.

They rode on in silence.

Herb Allen lived in a white house beginning to be in need of a coat of paint; it sat by itself on a slight rise of ground, at the north end of town, where buildings were scattered and the street lost its identity, becoming again the main road that

168

followed Colton Creek down through the valley. A big pine tree towered above the house, and there was the usual complement of outbuildings, privy and woodshed, and a tiny stable where the doctor probably kept his riding horse.

The doctor himself was working on his root crop, in a wired-off plot to the side of the house. The blade of a hoe flashed rhythmically as he bent and straightened, making his way along the rows. He was a tall, angular man in his middle years, full-bearded and vigorous; the way he went at his gardening suggested that it was, as much as anything, to give him exercise and keep in trim. He had worked up a sweat. When he saw he had callers he left his work and walked over to the fence, trailing the hoe and bringing out a colored bandana to mop his face.

"A shooting accident, Doc," Bob Ingram told him. "You're needed bad."

"Who got hurt?"

"Willie Ryker." Which wasn't actually a lie, of course, though the bullet burn on Willie's arm was slight enough that he could probably get over it without any doctor so much as having a look.

Allen asked no time-wasting questions. He was rolling down his sleeves as he said,

"I'll get my bag. Will you put this in the shed for me?" He handed over the hoe he had been working with.

"I'll saddle up for you, too," Bob Ingram said. "Don't want to lose any time." He turned his horse and headed for the stable on the other side of the house; passing Bannister, he gave the latter a look and got his nod of approval.

Allen gave the big stranger no more than a glance as he walked to the house and inside. Bannister had deliberately hung back, always just as happy to make himself as inconspicuous as possible. Now, as he waited, he stepped down and lifted the saddle fender for a look at his cinch. He undid the latigo, jerked it tight and reknotted it. He was just finished with this when he heard the sound of horses travelling the road below him.

Caution made him lead his mount the few steps to the cover of the big pine; there he watched as a group of riders came into view, riding south into town. He counted eight, and instantly recognized Russ Quint's blocky shape at their head. He tensed, knowing that he was not really hidden and that a casual glance from one of those Hatchet riders, as they passed below the Allen house, could easily spot him.

But to move was even more apt to draw attention and so he stayed as he was, holding the dun motionless; and the riders went on by at an easy, ground-eating lope. He thought in fact that one of the last in line did turn his head and look directly at him; he saw the dim blur of the face shaded by a pulled-down hatbrim, and he stiffened, expecting to hear a yell of warning to alert the rest. But then they were gone, riding on into the cluster of buildings along the creekbank that made up the town, and he reminded himself that a man usually sees only what he expects to see.

That rider had looked right at him and not noticed him at all, there by the thick trunk of the pine.

Allen's stable was a mere shed, with stalls and mangers for a couple of horses; apparently the doctor kept only one, a black gelding. When Bannister joined Bob Ingram there, the young fellow had the bridle and saddle in place and was just cinching down. He paused to listen, with a startled expression, as Bannister reported what he had just seen. "Whatever you do, you don't want to go through town, not with that many Hatchet riders here."

"No problem," Bob said. "We'll just ease

over this hill behind us. There's a good trail we can pick up, heading southwest. I'll tell the doc it's a shortcut. No reason anyone should see us."

"I'll watch to make sure." Bannister added, "You know, sooner or later Allen is going to start wondering just where you *are* taking him. It'll be up to you to satisfy his curiosity."

"Don't worry about that," young Ingram assured him firmly. "He's not going to get away from me, after we've gone to all this trouble, not if I have to knock him out and tie him to his saddle."

After that he was leading his own horse, and the doctor's, over to the house, as Allen emerged wearing a hat and jacket and carrying his instrument bag. He seemed to accept without much question young Ingram's explanation of the route they would be taking, with no more than a shrug he turned to lift his gaunt frame into the saddle and hang his bag on the pommel.

Bob Ingram had already mounted; now he reined over to where Jim Bannister stood beside his own animal. Looking down at the tall stranger, he said soberly, "If I'm not going to be seeing you again I just want to say thanks."

He reached down a hand; Bannister shook it briefly. "All right," he said, and stepped back while Bob pulled his horse around and went to rejoin the doctor.

Bannister watched the pair of them ride together toward the low rise that backed the creek, climb it and drop from view beyond. His own thoughts were already ranging ahead, working at the vaguely defined purpose that had brought him down here with Ingram. Though it had been no more than a dim notion, the sight of Quint and a large segment of the Hatchet crew here in town, away from the ranch, made it suddenly appear a little more feasible.

As he was turning to find the stirrup, a startling sound drew his attention toward the road.

Past his horse's shoulder he sighted a familiar-looking pair of horsemen. Though he could not see their faces, he knew them for Hatchet riders, part of the group that had ridden past into town a few moments earlier. These two had turned back; and now, as he watched, they pulled aside into the doctor's lane that led up the hill directly for the place where Bannister was standing.

There was still time, barely, and he did the only thing he could. Still watching the riders, he backed the few paces to the horse shed, drawing the dun after him. Inside, he put the animal into one of the two stalls and then edged over by the door. He held back in the shadows, where dust motes swirled before his face in a pencil of light streaking through a crack in the siding, and waited to see what the two men from Hatchet wanted.

They came up into the yard and halted, looking the place over. One lifted a yell at the house, "Doc! Doc Allen!" They listened for an answer, while the wind along the slope sang in the boughs of the big pine. Hearing none they conferred a moment. Then one gave his horse a kick and sent him deeper into the yard, along the side of the house.

His companion called after him; "He ain't here, Milt. Where the hell you going?"

Milt answered over his shoulder: "I'm just going to check and see if his horse is in the shed."

Bannister's jaw firmed and he slid his gun from the holster, holding it ready as Milt came on, straight toward him.

And then the second man swore impatiently. "What the hell, you gonna ask the *pony* to dig that rock out of your face?

Look! You've stood it this long, you can wait a little longer. And Russ Quint won't! He's got his orders, too. You know the pressure Dorsey's putting on him."

The approaching rider had halted, half turning his head to listen to his companion; this gave the man in the stable a look at Milt's face. One whole side looked raw and pitted with many small, bloody wounds. Suddenly Bannister remembered the bullet that struck a granite boulder during that morning's gunfight on the ridge, how it kicked up a glittering cloud of mica chips, and how the Hatchet crewman had dropped his gun and fled blindly, clutching at his face.

Apparently the bits of stone embedded deeply in his flesh were still bothering him.

But if he wanted Herb Allen to tend to his cuts, and pick the remaining shards from his flesh and treat the wounds with disinfectant, he apparently saw it would have to be another time. He shook his head, cursed thinly, and gave the reins a savage yank that whipped his horse about to rejoin the other rider. They went back down to the road, and turning right were presently lost to Bannister's view.

Only then did he relax, breathing deeply a time or two to ease the cramping tightness in his chest. He let the six-shooter off cock and holstered it. Afterward, leading the dun out of the shed, he quickly mounted up. Cautiously walking his horse down to the road, he checked to make certain no Hatchet rider was in sight. Afterward, putting his back to the village, he gave the dun the spur and sent it northward at a ground-eating lope.

He felt easier when the town, and Russ Quint's riders, were well behind him, with the trail to Hatchet lying empty as it followed the rushing course of the creek.

Flat on his belly behind a screen of brush, elbows propping the glasses in front of his eyes in a position that would prevent the noon sun from flashing on the lenses, Jim Bannister gave the ranch headquarters below him a patient and careful scrutiny. It appeared deserted, and that seemed almost unbelievable even though it was what he had hoped for. With an operation the size of Hatchet, even in the very busiest of seasons you would still expect to find some of the crew at work around the home buildings.

He could see nothing of the sort, however, though he watched the barn and the two bunkhouses with special care to catch any hint of movement that might be visible through doors or windows. Smoke drifted from the tin-pipe chimney of the kitchen where the ranch cook seemed to be holding the fort by himself; otherwise, after twenty minutes' inspection he had to conclude that the whole of Hatchet's crew seemed to have been drawn off elsewhere.

There was only one explanation. Like the bunch he had seen in town with Russ Quint, they had all been sent on the search for Nat Hardman, or for the drifter who presumably knew where he was. Bannister was willing to wager that all the normal activity of the ranch had been suspended, in this emergency.

And then he saw that the cook was not entirely alone. The door of the big house had opened and someone walked out onto the veranda. Bannister caught the movement, and at once he put the glasses to his eyes and came in on it. It was the woman; she had moved out to the edge of the steps. There she lifted a hand against a roof pillar, and stood looking about the yard and then to the hills beyond the ranch. For an instant she seemed to look straight at Bannister; he had to quell an impulse to lower the glasses and hastily duck his head. He could see her face clearly, and almost, he thought, read the unhappiness that he knew was there.

At length, she lowered her arm and turned away, moving slowly and dispiritedly. He watched till she had gone inside the house and the door closed behind her; he nodded shortly, in satisfaction.

He had made a lucky guess, but no telling how much longer he could count on his luck when this inspection had already used up precious time. Feeling the pressure, he inched back from his hiding place, got to his feet and went down the hill to where he had left his horse.

With the glasses returned to their case on his saddle, Bannister rubbed a hand across the rasp of yellow whisker stubble. Though the disguise of a saddle drifter wouldn't serve him now, it was after all a time and place when almost any busy man might go a week without shaving. He had brushed as much of the dried mud as he could from his battered denims, and taken a clean shirt and neckcloth from his pack roll. He ran his fingers through the tangle of tawny hair lying in full wings on either side of his head, and decided he was ready to try to convince the woman in the house that he was someone not to be frightened of.

He kept a cautious wariness as he rode in toward the buildings, but the horses in a couple of corrals were the only moving things he saw. He rode directly toward the big house, with its windbreak of budding poplars, and dismounted at the same hitching rack where he had tied up last night. Wrapping the reins, he went up the broad steps and, not giving himself time to ask himself again if this would really work, twisted the bell knob in the center of the heavy door.

He had rather thought a housekeeper might answer, but when the door opened it was the woman herself who looked anxiously out at him. She couldn't have been sleeping well; there were smudges of strain beneath her eyes and her manner was distracted. Bannister felt a sudden surge of pity for her, at the same moment that he recognized again that she was an uncommonly goodlooking person.

There was mingled hope and dread and puzzlement in her eyes as she said, "Yes?"

He tried to reassure her. "Ma'am, I'm one of the new hands. I reckon you saw me last evening, talking to your husband and Mr. Quint and Mr. Tacker."

"Oh . . . yes." Apparently she did remember him, vaguely; it should make this easier.

He drew a breath, and plunged into it. "We've found your father, Mrs. Dorsey. Up in the hills."

The woman's eyes rounded in alarm. "He — he isn't — ?"

"No, ma'am," Bannister said quickly. "He's alive but he's hurt pretty bad, and we thought best not to move him. The doctor's already been sent for. Meanwhile, Mr. Hardman's asking for you. If you want, I can take you to him."

"Of course! I'll have to change. I won't be a moment." She added, looking at him closely, "What is your name?"

He had one ready. "Jim Bonner."

"Thank you so very much, Mr. Bonner. I've been nearly frantic!"

"I'm sure you have." His sincere feeling must have shown, for the smile she gave him held trust. Before she could turn away he added, "Can I saddle a horse for you?"

"Yes, please. It's the bay mare with the right front stocking. You'll find my gear in the tack room."

Bannister nodded, and returned to his horse as the door closed behind him. Riding to the corrals, he quickly spotted the bay, a docile but sturdy little horse. He used a rope he found hanging on a post; the animal gave no trouble as he caught it up and snubbed it to the fence, while he hunted for the tack room.

Sarah Dorsey's saddle was easy enough to identify, light and ornamented with designs burnt into the leather, her initials worked into the stirrup fender. As he got the gear onto the mare, Bannister kept an eye on the closed door of the kitchen. Cow-ranch cooks that he had known often had an uncanny memory for names and faces and, even on a big spread like this one with a constant turnover of crew, were able to spot immediately someone who didn't belong. But he got the job done without interference, and rode back to the house leading the bay.

He was starting up the steps again when Sarah Dorsey came out. She had changed to a dark riding skirt, and a blouse and corduroy jacket and round-brimmed hat, and a green silk scarf knotted at her throat. She was a little breathless with hurrying. She asked, "How far is it?"

"Kind of far," Bannister admitted. "But we'll move right along." He held the stirrup for her and she stepped up with easy grace, settled her skirts and took the reins. As he turned away she stopped him with an anxious word: "You haven't said . . . how was he hurt?"

She would know soon enough — know a great many things he wasn't prepared yet to tell her, because he doubted she would believe them from the mouth of a total stranger. He answered quietly, "I'm afraid your father was shot, Mrs. Dorsey."

"Shot!" She echoed it, in a tone of pure horror. Her mouth trembled. "Then it must really be true about his enemies! About those other ranchers who'll do anything to hurt him, and Hatchet. . . ."

"As for that," Bannister said, "why don't you wait and draw your conclusions after you've had a chance to hear from his own lips what happened?" Not trusting himself to say any more just then, because there was no reason to think she would believe him, he turned abruptly to his own horse.

Too late he heard the sound of an approaching rider. His head jerked about as Coleman Dorsey rode at a walk around the corner of the house, and hauled rein staring at him.

Chapter 12

In that first moment it would be hard to say who was the most taken by surprise. Bannister, acutely conscious of the woman's presence, checked the first impulse that would have sent a hand moving toward his gun. As for Coleman Dorsey, astonishment honed his stare and one could almost read the swift and puzzled speculations working behind his cold gray eyes. He was the first to speak.

He looked past the stranger to his wife, waiting in the saddle, and demanded, "Just what is going on here?"

She answered his question. "This man, Mr. Bonner, says that Papa's been found! Cole, he's been *shot!* He's too badly hurt to be moved, but Mr. Bonner can take us to where he is."

There was no expression in her husband's face. The cold stare sought Bannister again. "Yes, I'm sure he can," he said, and the iron was carefully hidden in his voice. He shifted position slightly; the skirt of his coat fell away, revealing the gunhandle jutting from his belt holster. His hand dropped toward it.

But the other man had seen his intention, and now Bannister's own weapon slid into the open. "Don't do it," he said sharply. "Just put both hands on the saddlehorn and keep them there!"

He saw the reckless urge to defy him, but Coleman Dorsey seemed to be someone who played the odds and refused to buck a pat hand. The cold eyes measured the chances; the wide mouth drew down, the blunt jaw hardened. "I don't seem to have much choice," Dorsey said, and very deliberately placed his hands where he had been told.

There was a startled sound from the woman. Moving back a step, so he could look at her without losing control of his prisoner, Bannister saw the bewilderment in her eyes. She said faintly, "I, I just don't understand!"

"No, ma'am." Bannister drew a long breath, reluctantly facing the explanation that he had hoped to avoid. "I wanted you to hear this from your father's own lips," he said, "because I know you aren't apt to believe it coming from me. The short of it is, Nat Hardman was shot by one of his own men, a fellow named Sid Tacker."

"It's a lie!" Coleman Dorsey snapped.

"I heard Tacker admit it." Bannister's attention was still on the woman, as he sought earnestly for the words that would convince her. "As I put it together, Mrs. Dorsey, your husband and Nat Hardman have had a falling out. Coleman Dorsey's been loading down the payroll with tough gunhands, men like Tacker and Russ Quint, brought in here on purpose to turn them loose against your neighbors. But at last your father put his foot down, and so, they shot him!"

The woman was staring at him, her face drained of color. Now she lifted her glance to her husband as the latter said, in great anger, "Sarah, there's no reason you should listen to this nonsense! Whoever he is, the man is obviously working for your father's enemies."

Bannister plowed ahead. "Mrs. Dorsey, I saw the two of you yesterday morning, up at Wolford's. Apparently your husband found some excuse to get you out of the valley and away from the ranch overnight, so his killers could have a free hand. Tacker was to be the executioner, only he bungled the job. When I stumbled across your father he was hurt but still alive, hiding from his own crew. He told me part of the story; the rest, I've been learning since."

"And quite a story it is!" Coleman Dorsey said with harsh contempt, though Bannister saw a tinge of heightened color in his flat cheeks, and knew how hard he had been hit. "You must really take my wife for a fool," he went on loudly, "to imagine she'd listen to such stuff on the word of some nameless saddle tramp! What's the game, anyway? Mort Woods, or those Ingrams, or whichever of that trash it was that hired you, are they counting on you to lead her into their hands to hold as a hostage against us?" He flicked an accusing glance at his wife, dressed for riding, obviously ready to follow the tall stranger wherever he might have taken her. He shook his head. "And it damn well looks as though the lie would have worked if I hadn't happened to show up!"

A little desperately, Jim Bannister insisted: "It was no lie, Mrs. Dorsey! You've got to believe I'm telling the truth!" But as he spoke, he saw how her expression closed down; her decision had been reached, and it had gone against him. She was, he thought, a very feminine woman, one who would be closely dependent upon whatever male dominated her life — her father, first of all, and now this husband. She needed that support. An outsider was not likely to reach her, or turn her away from it.

As she looked at Cole Dorsey, her whole manner was apologetic. "I'm sorry!" she exclaimed, on an indrawn breath. "But I've been waiting desperately for word of Papa and when he came. . . ." Her mouth drew out long with misery and the tears dimmed her eyes, and she began to cry. "I'm sorry."

"Very well." The man spoke crisply, with no trace of sympathy or pity. When he looked down again at Bannister, standing on the ground between them, he contemptuously let the other man see the triumph in his cold eyes. "And what do you think you're going to do now? Take us both away with you, perhaps, at gunpoint?"

For a moment Bannister actually considered it. But there was danger enough for him, traveling these hills, without taking on the burden of two unwilling prisoners. He swore under his breath, while the moment dragged out and the horses shifted restlessly.

And then he saw them.

A quick stab of brightness, sunlight flashing on harness metal, probably, caught his glance and whipped his head up. A mile or so distant across the rolling valley floor, a segment of the trail from the creek was visible as it crested a rise; there he glimpsed a group of horsemen, briefly, before the dipping of the land carried them down from sight again. It was enough. He knew those Hatchet riders would be here in a matter of minutes; whatever he did must be done fast.

Almost too late he heard movement that brought his attention again to Coleman Dorsey. The man thought he saw his chance. His arm was back, his hand clamped about gun butt and already starting to pull it from the holster, when a step brought Bannister to him. He reached up, trapped the man's wrist and jerked hard. Dorsey's mount sidled away, pulling him off balance. As he started to fall, Bannister simply lifted his own gun and chopped the barrel of it downward across the man's skull.

The hat broke the blow's force but it was enough. Dorsey gave a groan, his eyes rolled back and he went limp. Bannister stepped back, letting go of his arm. The hat dropped from Dorsey's head and he slid loosely off his horse and landed in a heap on the ground, as his terrified wife's scream sounded in Jim Bannister's ear.

Bannister shot a look toward the road. The approaching riders were not yet in sight and he doubted if the woman's scream would have carried that far; but it would surely have reached to the kitchen shack. He didn't wait to find out. Jamming the gun into the holster he turned, quickly snatched the dun's reins free of the hitching pole and swung astride.

He looked at the woman, saw her staring at her husband lying motionless on the ground, her face pale as death. She seemed stunned, and there was no response when he kneed his horse close to hers and said, "Come along!" Bannister simply gave the mare's rump a whack with the flat of his hand. It leaped forward. Sarah Dorsey's head jerked on her shoulders but with a horsewoman's instinct she adjusted to the animal's lunging start. And Bannister kicked the dun into motion.

They left Coleman Dorsey beside his motionless horse. When they reached the corner of the house, Bannister rammed the mare with his mount's shoulder and turned it. They ran along the side of the building, shadows of the poplars flickering above them, the house itself hiding them from the kitchen. Anytime the little mare started to falter, Bannister gave it a flick with his rein ends. The woman herself seemed almost in a trance, unaware of what was happening.

But when a fold of the ground put the ranch buildings out of sight, Bannister pulled up for a moment, catching hold of the mare's headstall to draw it to a stand while he got his bearings. And now Sarah Dorsey lifted her head and looked about her, and as her eyes touched Jim Bannister they widened in quick revulsion. "You *killed* him!"

He shook his head. "No, ma'am. I didn't hit him hard enough for that. I just wanted to put him out of the way for the moment." If all he suspected about Coleman Dorsey was true, he would have been justified in shooting the man out of hand when he tried to pull his gun. But the sound of shots would have carried too well to those approaching Hatchet riders and anyway, you couldn't kill a man, not even that man, with his wife looking on. Coleman Dorsey would have to wait for the punishment he deserved.

Sarah Dorsey demanded, in a voice that shook with loathing and terror, "And now what do you plan to do with *me?* Kill me, too? Or hold me for a hostage?"

Sympathy for her plight forced patience

on him. "Mrs. Dorsey, I intend to do just what I said, take you to see your father. If we're in luck, and he's still alive, then maybe he can make you see the truth of what's been going on; I know *I* can't! I only wish, for now, you could try to believe I'm not your enemy. I want to help you!"

Her eyes left his face, wandered to her hands that were clenched on the reins. "How can I possibly believe that?"

"Don't then!" His jaw tightened. "But you're coming with me. If I have to, I can tie you in your saddle." And reluctantly he laid his hand on the rope that he had brought with him from the corral, for just that purpose if it proved necessary.

Sarah Dorsey looked at the rope. Her eyes were dulled by shock and despair; she shrugged, without spirit. "I suppose you'll do what you like."

"I'll take that as your word that you aren't going to try to escape," Jim Bannister said. "And I won't tie you." He shook his head. "If you could only understand how much I hate what I'm putting you through! But as I see it, Coleman Dorsey has got to be stopped; and you and your father are the only hope of doing it without God knows what kind of bloodshed. But first you've got to be made to see

191

what kind of man he really is, and that's all I'm trying to do."

He saw he was making no progress, and he gave up the effort. Taking the reins out of the woman's hands he turned his horse, leading the mare. They were in a gully that had been a watercourse and probably still carried runoff in wet seasons; its floor was littered with rock rubble that would take little sign, and it climbed sharply, into a stand of aspen in new leaf. Bannister led the way into the trees, pressing hard, the mare following docilely. Whatever her thoughts and emotions, Sarah Dorsey for the time being at least was keeping them to herself.

Having actually got away from Hatchet headquarters, Jim Bannister could breathe easier. But if he had been the center of a manhunt before, it was nothing compared to what he had started now. There would be no letup now that he had dared to kidnap Coleman Dorsey's wife.

He tried to take a look back, but by this time the contour of the land hid the ranch headquarters. So he plunged deeper into the crowded aspen, picking a way through them, and came out upon a grassy bench leading toward a rise that was studded with broken slant rock and pine. As they struck toward this, he wondered how long it would take Hatchet's riders to be hot on his trail.

In the first moment, Coleman Dorsey was only aware of his own head, bigger than the world, and throbbing with a blinding ache, and of the fire of whiskey burning in his throat and nostrils. He found he was coughing and slobbering and fighting for breath. When he got his eyes opened they were streaming with tears, and blurred impressions settled and became the whiskey bottle someone was holding in front of his face. Whoever had poured the stuff into him wanted to give him more, and he groaned and drew back and managed to raise a hand and push it from him. He heard his own voice say, between spasms of coughing, "Take that damn stuff away!"

But it had done the trick, however rudely, of reviving him after a fashion. He became aware that he was still sprawled in the dirt before the Hatchet ranch house, though someone had dragged him from under the feet of his horse and as far as the veranda steps. He was propped against them, able now to hold up his head even though it seemed to swell and subside again with each agonizing throb of heart-beat. And as other confused impressions sorted themselves out, and the world quit spinning, he made out the faces of his crew staring at him.

That angered him. The blow on the head that knocked him out had not addled his thinking; he remembered perfectly every-thing that happened, every detail of the scene that had ensued when he rode around the corner of the house and, without any warning, found Sarah together with the stranger. It all came rushing in on him, and with it came a great sense of ur-gency. "Damn you!" he told the blank faces looming over him; his own voice sounded muffled by the painful ringing that filled his skull, "Why are you standing there, gaping like idiots? Get after them!"

No one moved. It was Russ Quint holding the uncorked bottle; Quint said now, "After *who,* Cole? You better calm down and tell us what's going on. All we know, we come riding in and find you lying on your face, knocked cold. Looks like somebody bent a sixgun barrel over your skull."

"That's just what happened!" Dorsey snapped waspishly. "That drifter, that same fiddlefoot that's been giving us nothing but trouble! He rode in here bold as brass, knocked me out and made off with my wife!"

Quint stared. "Cole, that sounds absolutely crazy!" He broke off, seeming to quail a little at something that came into his employer's eyes.

"Crazy?" Dorsey roared back at him. "You think I don't know what I'm talking about?" He winced, and touched his hand to his head; he had to wait a moment to get himself under control. "They were both here. And you don't see them now, do you?"

"When did it happen?"

"How the hell do I know?" But when he squinted at the sun, he decided it couldn't have moved appreciably since the last time he saw it. "Not more than a few minutes ago, likely. Get these men scouting and see how fast they can pick up a trail."

Russ Quint, to his credit, could follow an order even when he didn't completely understand it. He barked a command, and it sent the crew into their saddles. Someone with sharp eyes had already been reading the medley of hoofprints in rain-softened dirt. "I think this way," he shouted, and after a certain confused milling the rest were after him like a pack hunting the scent.

Quint turned back to his employer, who had pushed himself up to a sitting position. "Give me that bottle," Dorsey grunted. He took it and tilted it and helped himself to three or four good swallows, and when he lowered it again his head felt clearer even though it still threatened to burst apart like a ripe melon. Dorsey set the bottle on the step beside him and ran a palm across his mouth. His voice, when he spoke again, was considerably stronger, his thoughts more coherent.

"Now listen!" he said, with an intensity that drew Russ Quint close to hear what he had to say. "You've got to understand. That fellow Bonner has to be caught!"

Quint looked at him blankly. "Bonner?"

"Well, it's the name he gave my wife. Whoever he is, *whatever* he is, the man is no ordinary range tramp. That's the mistake we've all made from the beginning."

"Damn it, Cole," the other said, quickly defensive. "It's sure as hell what he looked like. And we caught him on a stolen horse. How would we think any different?"

"So everybody's talked in front of him," Dorsey went on bitterly. "As though it didn't make any difference at all how much he heard or knew! He heard Sid Tacker brag about being the one who shot Nat, no telling what else. The result is that he either knows, or has guessed, a damn sight more than is safe. What's more, he's told Sarah the whole yarn. So far, she doesn't believe him. But unless we stop him, he's taking her straight to the old man!"

Quint had a sulky look, but he knew better than to argue with Dorsey in that mood. "We'll stop him," he promised grimly. And then Nels McPhee was back, reining his horse down hard as he reported excitedly, "We're onto their trail, all right! They're no more than minutes ahead of us."

"Be right with you," Quint told him, and looked again at his employer. The latter had reached up and hooked a hand over the railing, and was hoisting himself to his feet. "You coming too, Cole?"

But Coleman Dorsey shook his head as he half-leaned, half clung to the railing, gasping with blinding pain. He said harshly, "No, go ahead. I'd only hold you up." He put a hand to his head, and the knot that the gunbarrel blow had built there. "I'm charging you to get the man who did this to me! Don't take any more chances with him. When you see him, kill him."

Russ Quint stared. He opened his mouth

to say, *But if we do, how we going to find Hardman?* Killing the drifter out of hand, before making him reveal the old man's whereabouts, could endanger all of Cole Dorsey's careful schemes. Surely he saw that. Or was it the pain in his head doing the talking, just then?

Quint wished he could be sure. He had known Coleman Dorsey quite a long while. It went back half a dozen years to their meeting in a Denver gambling joint, when he'd recognized the cold-eyed stranger as someone with brains and hard ambition and an eye for the main chance, and had attached himself to the tail of Dorsey's kite.

But in these years, he'd more than once detected in the man hints of something that puzzled him, a blackness, an irrationality that could crop up briefly and startlingly in moments of stress. He had learned it didn't pay to call attention to these lapses, for fear of letting loose on his head a burst of alarming and violent rage. It was better to hold his tongue and watch, and wait, handling Dorsey with caution until the storm blew over and the air cleared.

Well, certainly the man had taken some bad blows in these past hours, the word yesterday of Hardman's escape from

Tacker and the others assigned to kill him; the maddening interference by the stranger they'd obviously been wrong to take for a mere saddle tramp; not least, the way those damned Ingram brothers had managed to escape from the trap this morning, with the help of an unseen rifleman, most likely one of Mort Woods' crew. Now, the kidnapping of his wife and the gun-barrel blow must have been one too many.

Surely when his head cleared, even Dorsey would see he had been acting irrationally. But for the moment Quint knew, from hard experience, that there was no point in arguing. He nodded, mumbling something, and turned quickly to his waiting horse.

Chapter 13

On the chase again, Bannister found that this time his instinct to seek high ground over his pursuers was thwarted by the terrain. When he had been pushing the laboring horses for the better part of an hour, clambering up every possible defile and ravine, he suddenly reined up and swore under his breath as he saw that further gain was blocked. There had been a fault slip, in some past eon, that now stretched an unmountable barrier of bare slick rock above him in either direction, a wall rising above the spears of timber that showed him no break anywhere.

He scowled as he puzzled over the problem, and looked at the woman.

Sarah Dorsey had long since recovered from her first dazed shock. The sheer work of staying in saddle, responding to the laboring movements of the mare, must have helped. Her cheeks had lost their pallor and were flushed with effort; her brown hair, done up in a hasty coil beneath the flatbrimmed riding hat, had come undone and hung untidily about her face, but it did not detract from her healthy good looks. Bannister had been a little surprised that she made no effort to escape while his hands were full negotiating the climb; even with her horse's reins imprisoned, she could still have found plenty of chances to slip from its back. But she must have known it was futile and that he'd have been after her at once; still, she could have caused a bad delay, giving the Hatchet riders a better chance of catching up with them.

He let himself wonder if she could possibly be having second thoughts about him, thinking she ought to give him a chance to prove whether the story he had told her was true. But when he looked in her face he saw nothing to encourage him. She pushed the hair from her eyes with the back of a wrist, and returned his look coldly. It pleased her to know he was in trouble.

More than likely, she knew these hills at least as well as any of her husband's crew, but plainly there was no use asking her for help. With a jerk of the head Bannister said curtly, "We'll try this way," and turned their horses south along the foot of the fault scarp. Sarah Dorsey still said nothing at all.

Both mounts were beginning to show the hard travel. Bannister's dun had covered a lot of miles since morning and the sweat was dark on its straining flanks; for the little mare, too, bucking these steep and rubble-littered slants was no easy task. Presently they fell into a game trail, skirting the scarp's base, and this made things a little easier. Still, he couldn't run their mounts into the ground. He had to let them halt ever more frequently to rest.

In these intervals he would test the unbroken stillness about him. And it was now that the woman's continued refusal to communicate began to get on his nerves.

She might be putty in the hands of her husband, but there was a passive, stubborn streak in her as well and it was this side she was showing Bannister. He gritted his teeth over his failure to convince her he meant her no harm but was in fact risking his neck for her in a fight that was not really his concern. She completely exasperated him; he told himself he must be a fool to bother.

Except that he wasn't forgetting his own score against Cole Dorsey's tough crew; the beating, the noose around his neck, the dragging at the end of a rope.

Where a fairly steep slope dropped away

to their left, studded by boulders and a scatter of stunted timber, a movement glimpsed through the lower trees made him pull to a halt suddenly. Now he could hear the sound of horse travel that had been masked by the noise made by their own animals. Now, bending in the saddle, he peered down through the screen of twisted trunks and branches and saw a line of a half dozen riders, following another trail that paralleled their own, some hundred yards below them.

The breath caught in his throat and he felt for his holstered gun, his thoughts racing. It appalled him that after all his effort, the pursuers should be so close! There was no way to go but straight ahead, but what would happen if the two trails should converge, somewhere up ahead?

At least they didn't seem aware of the nearness of their quarry. They rode with heads down, all attention on the trail their animals were negotiating. No one looked up the rise; if they did, Bannister was hopeful they would miss the pair holding motionless among the tree trunks.

Then, at his elbow, Sarah Dorsey's voice lifted in a cry that shrilled across the hush of the mountainside: "I'm up here! Help, *please help me!*"

Furious, Bannister whirled on her. Too late. He managed to clamp a hand over her mouth, but then he had to drop the reins and seize her by a shoulder as she fought him. The damage had been done. Down below, shouts lifted. The horses moved about uneasily, adding to his difficulties. The woman struck at him, her fist stinging his cheek. He swore and tightened his grip.

She bit the palm that covered her mouth. He wasn't expecting that and the next moment she was able to break free. Bannister made a grab but the cloth of her jacket slid between his fingers. Somehow, then, she had caught the reins of the mare and was yanking it away, turning its head downhill.

Bannister yelled after her but she was already gone, plunging straight down the slope, with reckless determination now that she was free. Jaw set, seeing everything falling apart, Jim Bannister set out in her wake. It was the most treacherous footing. The dun slipped, caught itself again. A jagged boulder seemed to leap toward them but a wrench at the reins altered their course. A wind-twisted tree raked a branch across the arm he flung up to protect his face.

But the little mare was sure-footed and the woman desperately bent on escape, and he could not seem to gain on her. Below, he saw that the Hatchet riders had heard her cry and now were coming up to meet them, threading a way among the trees and boulders.

Then the bay mare squealed in terror as it lost footing and went down heavily on both knees. Sarah Dorsey was flung against the saddlehorn, almost pitched forward over her animal's head. By the time she managed to right herself, Bannister had closed the distance. A reach and a grab took the reins away from her; the dun went onto its haunches, sliding and almost slamming into a tree. Bannister got it turned then, kicked it with the spur. Powerful muscles bunched and surged; the mare was yanked back to her feet and both horses were starting to climb again.

One of the riders below them yelled something and a handgun barked. He was trying to miss the woman and hit Bannister, and so his shot was wide, the bullet striking a boulder in screaming ricochet. But it was enough to tighten the muscles of Bannister's shoulders and make him kick the dun into harder effort. There was a second shot, a third; they seemed to come from different guns at random. Bannister found himself thinking, *They don't give much of a damn if they do hit her!*

Then they had scrambled back to the trail, and with surer footing under them the horses leaped forward. Moments later they flashed into a cut between a pair of tumbled slabs of rock, and the enemy was left behind them. Bannister, looking at his companion, saw at once that her mare was stumbling badly, its forelegs bleeding from the tumble it had taken. The woman herself, he thought, was close to hysteria; her reserves of courage had been exhausted and he could see she was crying as she clung to the saddle, blinded by the tears that wet her face.

He knew the bay was only minutes away from going lame; it could travel no further. Nor would the dun be able to carry them both. That last scramble, in the loose rubble of the hillside had told on it. The animal was laboring, its sides lathered with dust-coated sweat. Jim Bannister shook his head, feeling the pressure of a desperate situation: his enemies close at his back, and no good options left him.

They were in more timber, thicker-growing here, where a fold in the mountain face led drainage down from the higher reaches. Many of the trees were good-sized spruce and pine, but storms had torn up the shallow roots of some of them, creating a jackstraw tangle of blow-downs that clogged the throat of the ravine. The trail dropped away, skirting the lower edge of this thicket; above, a stretch of rimrock showed, pitted with the dark erosion hollows. Bannister took all this in with a sweeping glance, and out of necessity reached his decision.

In a moment he was out of the saddle, and with his hands at the woman's waist hauled her down from her own. A slap on the rump of each of the horses sent them clattering on, though in their present shape he knew they would likely not go far. Not giving Sarah Dorsey time to stammer a question, he seized her by an arm and shoved her ahead of him. At this point a good-sized spruce had been toppled and partly sunk into the litter of the hillside; Bannister made the woman scramble across the fallen trunk and into the hollow made when its roots tore free. Packed solid with stones and dirt, the root system reared a massive shield and Bannister pushed the woman in under this, and dropped prone beside her.

They were barely in time. The racket of running horses grew louder, spattering off the slabs of rock that bracketed the trail, abruptly ending as the riders pulled their animals to a halt. Someone shouted, "There!" and another answered, "No, that's only the broncs. They've turned them loose." The voices dropped to a murmur and Bannister knew they were discussing this development; he also knew the delay would not last long.

Now the horses were in motion again, bringing their riders along the trail toward the place where Bannister and the woman lay hidden. His breath shallow, he waited to hear them pass. He stiffened when, at a command, they all pulled rein instead, so close beside the fallen spruce that the blowing of horses, and the jingling of a bit chain, were clearly audible. They could not be a dozen feet away.

Bannister heard Sarah Dorsey's sudden intake of breath, and took warning. Remembering the outcry that had brought his enemies to him, he moved quickly to pin her with his own weight; he clapped one hand roughly over her mouth and drew his six-gun with the other. Tensely, then he waited.

One who appeared to be the leader — his voice sounded like Sid Tacker's — had reached a decision. "They're hiding in there somewhere. We got no choice, somebody has to go in and root them out."

"Oh, hell, Sid!" someone objected. "That stuff is treacherous. Bucking it, a bronc can snap his legs like matchsticks!"

"Then you'll have to go afoot," Tacker snapped back. "After all, *he* is. But remember, he's got a gun. Watch what you're doing, don't let him come on the blind side of you. Dutch, you take care of the horses. And keep *your* eyes open, too. We don't want the bastard sneaking back to pick one off for himself. Now, move."

They did. Bannister with the woman's breath warm against the hand clamped upon her mouth and his grip tight on the buttplates of his gun, heard a confusion of noises and talk as men stepped down from saddles and turned over the reins to the horse-holder. Boots went trampling into the undergrowth above the trail, blundering bodies began to smash their way through close-growing branches, hunting. He expected at any moment to be discovered, but the search was in some manner shunted around the base of the fallen spruce tree. It moved on. Rather quickly the sound of broken branches and trampling boots, and of voices calling back and forth, withdrew deeper into the timber.

Jim Bannister eased the air from

cramped lungs. But he was not out of danger yet and he held his place. Now someone, it would have to be Dutch the horse-holder, spoke within a few feet of him. "Sid, that drifter's too damn slippery. They'll never chase him out of there!"

"If they don't," Sid Tacker answered him, "if he does get away from us, just once more, Cole Dorsey is going to have all our hides nailed to the barn, in a row! Cole ain't a patient man, the best of times, and things just now ain't exactly going like be planned them."

The other retorted, "Well, don't look at *me!*" And next moment Bannister felt the woman stiffen against him as Dutch added, "If you'd only done the job right on old man Hardman, none of this would be happening."

It got him a furious cursing from Tacker. "The next loud-mouth throws it up to me about Nat Hardman, is going to get some teeth knocked down his throat! All right, so he got away — but I nailed him! Despite anything Cole or anyone else tells me, I still say the old bastard's dead."

"But you don't *know* it, and we still ain't found him. And now it looks like we got to go back and tell the boss that drifter's made off with his wife!"

"By God, no!" Tacker's tone was fierce. "We'll find them, and we'll find Hardman! There's plenty of places we ain't hunted yet. Right now I'm looking at those holes, up there. The rimrock's riddled with them, in places. Occurs to me, Hardman might have found him one somewhere, and crawled into it to hide."

He was interrupted by a shout from somewhere off back in the scrub, one of the crew seemed to think he had found something. Saddle leather creaked as Tacker hastily dismounted. Bannister heard him tell Dutch, "Look sharp, now!" And then he was off, on foot, making his way into the thicket to join his men who were calling back and forth as they tried to learn if someone had actually had some luck.

Bannister felt warm moisture on the back of his hand; he looked at the woman and saw her eyes were squeezed tight and her cheeks wet with tears. When he took his hand from her mouth she shook her head and whispered, with a look of misery, "I'm sorry! I should have believed you all along, but I just couldn't!"

All he could do to comfort her was squeeze her shoulder briefly. There was time for nothing more. If he hoped to get them out of their predicament, this was the only chance he was apt to have.

He whispered, "Stay put!" A quick look assured him his six-shooter was free of dirt and ready for use. Holding it, he backed cautiously out of the hollow where they had hidden, pressed together in the loose dirt with the roots of the fallen tree over their heads. He lay prone against the log for a moment, listening. There were the small sounds made by a half dozen horses, tearing at leaves and available tufts of grass, saddle gear creaking to their movement. Carefully, Bannister raised his head for a look.

Dutch was a slat-lean man, with a tough cast to this dark-bearded face. He had dismounted to ease his muscles while he waited; his own horse, a gray, stood on trailing reins but he was holding the leathers of the other five animals. He was turned partly away from Bannister, showing him a three-quarter profile, head canted, scowl searching the timber higher up for any sign of what his fellow crewmen might be accomplishing.

Jim Bannister rose to his knees. He said quietly, "All right, Dutch."

The man froze. The well-polished wooden handle of a Colt revolver stuck from the holster strapped to his right leg, and the last thing Bannister wanted right now was gunplay. "Don't do it!" he warned sharply.

It was already too late. Dutch had nerve and toughness; he wouldn't let himself be taken that easily. Suddenly he had flung the held reins aside and was twisting about in his tracks, going into a crouch as he pawed out the gun from its holster. Bannister had him covered but he was so reluctant to use it that he held his fire, and let the other get off the first shot.

It was aimed at the sound of his voice, and fired before Dutch was into position. Still, it came close enough that he flinched, and then, almost by reflex, his own six-gun made answer. The two shots ran together, explosive and startling in the stillness. Dutch doubled forward and the hat popped from his head. The gun fell from his hand and, with a look of blank surprise on his face, he curled up and dropped on his side and lay still.

The knot of saddle horses had burst apart, with squeals of terror. Jim Bannister was already vaulting across the fallen trunk and he managed to get Dutch's horse and catch the reins before it was able to bolt; but his grab for a second mount was too late, hampered by the gun he still had in his fist. The animal jerked its head and snatched the bridle out of reach, and he let it go. Already, back in the timber, he could hear excited yelling and he knew he had only seconds. He called to Sarah Dorsey, urging her sharply; she came scrambling from the hiding place. When she saw the man he had killed she halted, staring. Impatiently, Bannister seized and all but flung her into Dutch's saddle, and then he was up behind her.

A couple of the Hatchet mounts had vanished into the lower brush and trees; the other three had paused and had not run very far before they stopped and turned to eye him warily. Bannister fired his gun twice more, over their heads, and they whirled away and ran on from sight.

He didn't suppose it would take the Hatchet riders long to catch those mounts; he could only hope that it would give him the time he needed. He could have solved the problem, of course, by shooting the horses. But Jim Bannister had been a horse rancher, before the conflict with a corrupt syndicate agent lost him his spread and turned him into a fugitive. What he had seen of human nature, in the months since then, had only increased his preference for

214

horses. He would rather kill a man than his mount, if he thought the man deserved it; the horse he rode surely didn't.

Pouching the gun he told the woman, "Let's get out of here!"

The yelling and thrashing in the scrub was growing louder. Despite the shock of what she had just been through, Sarah Dorsey was sufficiently in control to respond. As Bannister put an arm around her waist she spurred the gray and it leaped forward. Moments later a twist in the trail left that place behind.

Chapter 14

Well aware that Tacker's bunch might not be the only Hatchet riders searching these hills, Jim Bannister was as wary of the trail in front of them as of the danger at their backs. So, when suddenly he heard the nicker of a horse, somewhere just ahead, he reacted instantly. He took the reins from the woman's hand at the same time drawing his gun.

Then the gray carried them over a brushy hump of ground, and the breath broke from him as he saw his own dun gelding standing by the trail, head lifted. There was no sign of the mare, but he supposed it would eventually straggle home to the Hatchet corral, lame, it could be no use to them now. The dun looked in good enough shape, though, with saddle and gear intact. Even though the animal was far from fresh, it beat riding double on the gray.

He dismounted quickly. The dun seemed glad to see him. He gave its flank a friendly slap as he checked the cinch. Also he took time to shorten the gray's stirrups. Stepping back, he looked at the woman.

Sarah Dorsey had been crying, silently, head down and shoulders drooping. When Bannister placed a hand on her wrist she showed him a face that was wet with tears and pale with grief. "Look," he said gruffly, "this is a mighty bad time for you. I wish you didn't have to learn the truth about Cole Dorsey, but there it is. At least now, maybe, you'll believe that I'm really trying to get you to your father."

She looked at him miserably, and nodded. "How far is it?"

"I don't know the country well enough to tell you. But maybe you'll recognize a half dome, the face of it sheared off smooth, and rising higher than the peaks around it." At her nod he added, "The place is just a little south of there, a natural cave high in the rimrock."

"I see." She hesitated, "What I don't understand is why you're putting yourself through all this for strangers! Of course," and she looked at his battered and bearded face and his worn clothing, "if Papa's promised you money, naturally we'll be glad to pay. Anything in reason."

Bannister stiffened; his hand dropped from her arm and he said coldly, "That won't be necessary. There's no payment involved." He let her see how angry he was as he turned away, abruptly, and swung onto the back of the dun.

He pushed on, as hard as he dared, relying on the woman's horsemanship to keep up. Sarah Dorsey seemed to be having no trouble with the gray. She'd probably ridden it before, since it wore the Hatchet brand and was plainly a part of the ranch string. There was no chance for more talking. As the horses scrambled over slick rock and passed through the thin shadow of timber stands, Bannister kept part of his attention on the backtrail, at the same time watching for anything familiar to show him where he was.

A thought had been nagging at him, and while they stopped to rest the horses he brought it up, but he spoke stiffly, still resentful of the woman's last comment. "Russ Quint's no fool. He knows I'm a complete stranger here, and that I probably only know the one route to your father's hiding place. He could send Tacker and part of the crew to drive us, and pick us off if they can, while he cuts ahead and waits someplace where he knows we'll have to pass."

Sarah Dorsey, standing beside the gray,

was taking advantage of the moment to do something about her hair, rolling it and tucking it under the brim of her hat. Arms lifted, she paused to consider this. "Then what are we to do?"

"I've been thinking. After I left Wolford's yesterday, I didn't follow the wagon road all the way. By accident I came across an old horse trail, that looked as though it might have been used before the new road was hacked out. I wonder if you know about it."

"Why, yes. That trail was meant for packing in supplies, when there still wasn't any way for getting a wagon in. Not many people even remember but Papa pointed it out to me, once."

Bannister asked, "Could we reach it from here? That way, if there's an ambush we could ride around it, come in on the cave from above."

She thought it over. "I remember Papa saying the old trail stayed high, after crossing the pass, because the only route for it to reach the valley was to come down through Jawbone Canyon. It means we'd still have to climb, almost to timberline. But I think I know a place, a few miles ahead."

"You lead," Bannister said. He helped

her to her saddle, mounted the dun and fell in behind.

Any doubt he had of her quickly vanished. She struck out at once, with a sureness that told him she really knew exactly where she was going. After so many hours of blindly fighting his way, he was glad enough to turn things over to her. Meanwhile, remembering that his gun had three used shells in it, he took the opportunity to get it out and, as he rode, punch out the empties and replace them from his belt.

Climbing, the way grew rougher and more than once crossed bare stretches of rock where, Bannister was sure, they left no sign that could be followed, so there was little danger now of leading Nat Hardman's enemies to him. At last they skirted a stand of scrubby timber growth and the old trail showed directly above them, hardly more than a scar across the weathered rock. Turning onto it, Bannister felt the worst was over.

The day was fast waning when they neared the spot where, so many long hours ago, Jim Bannister had stopped to investigate a horse standing motionless in the brush. Here they left the trail, and as they dropped down toward the cave young Bob Ingram was suddenly there in front of them, a rifle in his hands and a look of astonishment on his face.

"You almost got yourselves shot!" the young fellow exclaimed. "Riding in on me from *that* direction. How in the world — ?" And then speech failed him as he recognized the second rider.

Bannister turned to the woman. "You know Bob Ingram, I guess?"

Sarah Dorsey nodded. "Of course."

Though still plainly dumbfounded, young Ingram took this in stride. "Ma'am, I suppose Jim's filled you in on what's been going on. Old man —" he caught himself "— that is, your paw's inside. Doc's been working on him and says now he has a good chance." He turned to Bannister. "Doc says it's only thanks to you, though, managing to dig that bullet out."

Bannister felt the woman's frown searching his face. "You did that?"

"Somebody had to," he answered shortly, and dismounted. Reaching for her reins he told her, "You go in. I'll join you in a minute."

She let him help her down from the saddle. As good a horse-woman as she was, he knew it had been a very hard ride for her, and an emotional ordeal. He watched her make her way toward the low entrance of the cave, and then turned again to Bob Ingram. "No trouble for you and the doctor, getting up here?"

"He didn't like it much, when he found out I'd lied about how long a ride it was going to be. In fact he got his back up a time or two, until I finally told him who his patient really was, and how bad he'd been hurt. Like I told you, him and Nat Hardman are old friends. I'll take these horses, Jim."

"Thanks," Bannister said, passing him the reins. "And keep your eyes open. Use these." He indicated the glasses in the case hanging on his saddle. "Hatchet's scouring the hills. We can't let them catch us napping!"

"They won't," Ingram assured him. "It ain't too long till dark," he pointed out. "That should slow 'em down."

"Maybe."

The sun was already gone, and here in the hills that meant a short dusk, with shadows already beginning to collect in the hollows and timber thickets as the sky paled out to beaten steel. Bannister stood a moment testing the stillness, and watching Bob Ingram lead his horse and Sarah Dorsey's to put with the others. Finally, he turned and headed for the cave.

The aroma of coffee and frying bacon met him, reminding him that it was long hours since he'd eaten. The fire had been built against the rear wall of the shallow opening. Farley Ingram was on his knees working with skillet and turning fork, while Doc Allen waited, a tin plate in hand, for him to spear bacon onto it. Canned tomatoes stewed in a sauce pan, the coffee pot steamed in the coals. Willie Ryker squatted nearby with a neat bandage on his hurt arm and a tin cup in his hands, steam curling up before his face.

Sarah Dorsey was apparently uninterested in food. She sat close to where Nat Hardman lay with a blanket drawn over him for warmth. She had one of her father's hands clasped in both of hers. And this was the tableau that greeted Bannister as he ducked the low entrance, stepping into the hole in the rimrock.

For a moment no one moved. Then the woman said something to her father in a low voice, and the man beneath the blanket opened his eyes. His face was wan and drained, as though it had fallen in upon itself, but for the first time as he looked at Bannister his eyes were clear and reasonably free of the blindness of bullet shock and fever.

He said, in a voice that was weak but steady enough: "So you're the man who saved my life! It's the first real look I've had at you. For my own sake, and my daughter's too, I owe you a lot of thanks!" And he actually managed to bring up his other hand and extend it, trembling, toward the stranger.

The doctor, watching, said in alarm, "Nat! Easy! I warned you about using up your strength!"

Hartman shook his head. "I'm feeling pretty good, Herb. And I want this man to hear what I have to say. Bonner, is that it?" Bannister acknowledged the false name, face expressionless as he nodded. "From what my girl tells me," the hurt man continued, his voice taking on strength as he spoke, "you must be a pretty smart fellow, the way you figured things out after coming into this situation cold, a total stranger. For one thing, you saw right through that son-in-law of mine, when he had *me* completely fooled. I'll never forgive myself for urging Sarah to marry that scoundrel!"

"Papa! Hush!" the woman cried. "You mustn't blame yourself. Nobody could have made me marry him if I hadn't thought —" her voice broke "— I loved him!"

His head rolled, his eyes sought his daughter's face. He said in a tone of bitterness, "I seem to remember, when I first brought him to Hatchet, you said what impressed you was he was so much like *me!*"

"Oh, no, Papa! I just didn't know!"

"The hell of it is," he went on doggedly, "I think you were more right than you could have guessed. Cole Dorsey is ruthless and scheming and greedy, but so was I, not too many years ago. I told myself I was doing it for my family; but all I really wanted was to make Hatchet the biggest spread in this section of Colorado. And doing it, I didn't care who I hurt, or how much my neighbors came to hate me. It was your mother's dying, rest her soul!, that hauled me up short and brought home to me just what I'd been up to. And how empty it all was!

"But then Coleman Dorsey came into our lives," he continued, the bitterness deepening, "and took over without my really knowing it, or realizing how he was loading down the payroll with hired gunmen. When he finally came out in the open, with his talk about setting up a deadline to keep the other ranchers off their summer grass and once more making Hatchet a spread to be feared, I told him then that kind of thing was all in the past, and I'd never stand for it beginning again. I thought the whole thing had blown over but I see now, he was only biding his time."

Jim Bannister said, "Can you tell us exactly what happened, day before yesterday? What led to the shooting?"

"I was set up!" Hartman said. "Cole Dorsey concocted some reason why he had to be out of the valley overnight, and he took Sarah along; that gave his killer a clear field. But when Tacker and the others came looking for me, I got wind of what they had in their minds and I would have got clean away, except for that one unlucky bullet. I surely thought then I was done for. But I remembered that old trail and I made for it, and so, you happened to find me. I still can't get it through my head by what miracle that came about!"

"Call it blind luck," Bannister said shortly. He had been afraid of this question; he didn't want to discuss it, or start these people speculating, any more than they were already, as to just who he was, or what circumstances made him choose to travel obscure trails. He was frankly relieved when Farley Ingram picked this moment to bring him a plate of food and a cup of coffee. He settled down with it, on his haunches with his back against the rough wall of the cave, and as he ate he continued with the business at hand.

To the doctor he said, "When do you think it'll be safe to move him?"

"Not for awhile," Adams answered promptly. "His system wouldn't take it. That's a hard trip down from here even for a well man."

"I was thinking," Bannister said, "if I can rig up some kind of a horse litter, we might be able to haul him out over that old trail to Wolford's toll house. He'd be comfortable enough there. But we'll need daylight, so I guess he has to stay where he is till morning, at least." He drained off half of his cup of coffee. "So the question is, who's going to volunteer to stay with him?"

"Me, for one," the doctor answered promptly, to which the woman quickly added, "As long as there's anything I can do for Papa, I won't leave him."

The wounded man rocked his head from side to side in protest. "That ain't called for! I've put people to enough trouble already!"

"Don't be a damn stubborn fool *all* your life, Nat!" said Allen sharply. "I guess I know what's best for a patient. The wonder is, that you lived as long as you did with the bullet in you. I ain't letting you out of my sight until I'm satisfied you're free of danger."

And then, unexpectedly, the silent Willie Ryker put in a gruff word. "Speaking of danger," the old puncher said dryly, "I hope you ain't forgetting Cole Dorsey! After all the traffic to and from this cave, it ain't gonna be a secret much longer. Once Dorsey or them killers of his find it, there'll be hell busting loose around here! We best be thinking about getting help."

Farley Ingram suggested, "Mort Woods?"

The old man shrugged. "You can ask. But he'll say he's too damned busy watching the cattle you helped him move across the deadline, yesterday, to want any part of this fight. I know Mort!"

Jim Bannister set aside his empty cup and plate. "Any help we might be able to get," he said, "I have a hunch would come too late. We'd better be ready to make do with what we have!" He started to his feet.

The woman said, "Mr. Bonner."

"No, Mrs. Dorsey," he told her, curtly. "In case you're concerned about it, there still isn't any charge." He was still too out of sorts with her to want to get involved in another discussion. He turned away, to

Farley Ingram who had loaded another plate of grub. "Is that for your brother? I'll take it out to him." Ingram handed him the plate and cup and utensils.

To his back, Sarah Dorsey cried, "Won't you please give me a chance to apologize for saying what I did, Mr. Bonner? I know I was wrong, and I'm ashamed. What you've done was never for money, but out of the goodness of your heart. And I'd like to say I'm sorry!"

Slowly he turned to look at her. She made him feel contrite and somehow a little guilty for the way he'd been behaving. "It's all right," he told her, more gently. "Maybe it was only natural you'd think I was some sort of grubliner, hunting a handout." *If you act a role,* he thought, *don't be surprised if people believe it.*

"We'll just forget anything was said," he finished and got a wan smile in reply.

At the entrance he paused again, plate in hand, to look back at the fire blazing near the rear wall. "You'll do better without that," he told the group. "It's almost dark; and if anyone's looking for us, that could show up at night for a considerable distance."

The doctor shook his head. "I need the fire. Nat has to be warm."

Bannister considered, and shrugged. "Keep it small, then. Maybe it won't hurt anything."

Actually, when he had left the cave and looked back from a little distance, the glow of the fire, though visible, seemed faint. It had been built far enough back from the entrance, that one would have to look directly into the cave to have much of a view of it.

Grainy dusk lay over the hills, the sky still held a steely hint of light and no stars had as yet begun to show, but the shadows were deep and deceptive and he had to watch his step. With the plate of food in his hands, he called softly a time or two and got Bob Ingram's answer from a little to his left, about where he had expected. Bannister made his way there and found the young fellow leaning against a boulder, rifle cradled in his arms.

He was happy to see the food. "I was beginning to think they'd forgotten me," he told Bannister. He leaned his rifle against the side of the boulder and fell to work.

"Anything happening?"

The other answered with his mouth full: "Naw. A little while ago, I thought for a minute I heard something moving, down below, but it must have been an animal of some kind. In this dusk, you start thinking you see and hear all kinds of things that ain't there!"

Bannister explained what had been decided. "There seems no way to move Nat Hardman before morning, so we're all agreed to stay with him. Of course, we know Hatchet's looking high and low but if they haven't found him yet, they'll have to let up with nightfall. We'll keep a watch anyway, and worry about tomorrow when it gets here."

"All right," the young fellow said.

Next moment, he dropped the tin cup with a startling clatter. Somewhere below them the whicker of a horse had run shrilly across the stillness, ending abruptly, as though cut off by the pressure of an unseen hand.

Chapter 15

Bannister swore. Beside him young Ingram, tossing his plate away, snatched up the rifle and its tube rang a metallic note against the surface of the boulder. He said hoarsely, "They found us!"

"Sounds like it."

"It sure as hell wasn't one of our horses. They're up there in the hollow, with the hobbles on."

Jim Bannister didn't answer. He had drawn his gun and now he moved forward, setting his boots with caution. Ingram came crowding close at his heels. Keening the rising wind for further sound, he covered a hundred yards of the rough hillside before he signalled for a halt. They waited like that, searching the sweep of open ground and the tangles of thicket.

Bannister shook his head. "This is a mistake! You'd better get up to the cave, tell the rest what's happening in case they don't already know. Get that fire put out, and stand by with your guns ready."

"What about you?"

"Somehow, we've got to try to learn what sort of odds we're facing. I'm going to look around."

Bob Ingram, by this time, had fallen in the habit of taking orders from Bannister as though he sensed in him an authority, bestowed by his long months as an outlaw playing at this cat-and-mouse game. Now, the young fellow said merely, "All right, Jim," and turned away obediently. Bannister stood and listened to him climbing in the direction of the cave, whose mouth was just visible from here as a faint reflection of fireglow against rock.

Dusk lay like thick smoke, with treeheads rocking and underbrush rattling in a growing night wind, it was the most deceptive hour out of the twenty-four. Gun ready, Bannister went looking for his enemies.

The ground leveled presently, to become a shallow bench before it dropped away again. Here the growth thinned and he hauled up suddenly, his shoulder against a pine trunk, the breath gone shallow in his chest.

Someone was coming along the bench, moving lightly. Bannister caught the sound only moments before a hint of him shaped up in the gloom. Some ten yards distant he halted and Bannister tensed, thinking for a moment he had been discovered. He supposed the man had been sent up here hunting for a guard who might have to be surprised and disposed of. The buttplates of the six-shooter hard against his palm, Bannister waited.

For an agonizing time that other figure stood motionless, and his eyes began to water from staring too long into the grainy dusk. But now the man came on, beginning at last to take definite shape. Bannister was trying to decide whether to sing out a challenge when the man halted again, close enough that he definitely saw him turn and lift his head for a searching look up the face of the rise.

It was as good a chance at him as he was going to have. Bannister kept his voice down but let the threat of it carry. "Don't try to use the gun. You're covered."

There was a convulsive, bluffing movement and a gun flashed with muzzle fire, seemingly almost in his face. His answering shot was almost an instinctive reaction. The two explosions mingled, and then Jim Bannister was left standing, unhurt but with his vision smeared by bright after-image. Blinded, he heard but didn't see the other man topple to the ground, and then the echoes of that double clap of gunfire chased themselves into silence and he knew he was alone. There was no sound at all, not even a groan, from the one he had shot.

He moved forward until his boot touched a form that yielded limply. Going down on one knee, he examined the body gingerly. The man lay on his face, and when Bannister ran an exploring hand down the sleeve of his brush jacket he found the fingers still curled loosely around the butt of a six-shooter. He took the gun and tossed it aside, and then rolled the man onto his back.

The face showed palely but he wanted to know for sure who this was. After a moment's hesitation, he switched his revolver to his left hand and dug out a match, held it cupped in his palm as he snapped the sulfur alight on the buttplate of the gun. A single, quick look at the face of Sid Tacker, mouth fallen open beneath the rusty mustache, the staring eyes showing thin reflections of the match flame, was all he needed. Instantly he shook out the match and threw it away.

In almost the same moment, somewhere between him and the cave, he caught a murmur of startled voices and the sounds of a couple of men blundering in his direction. Bannister swore under his breath. *The Ingrams!* he thought. If they had let those gunshots lure them from their post. . . . With the next breath, another possibility struck him. It brought him to his feet, to fade back again into the clotted shadow of the pine, and there he waited as the pair approached.

They were almost within reach when one lifted his voice, calling cautiously. *"Sid?"* Not the Ingrams, then — Hatchet crewmen! Bannister froze: in another moment they would surely stumble upon Sid Tacker's body. But somehow they missed it, and went on along the bench at the same hurried prowl, a note of anxiety now in the voice that continued to call Tacker's name. He let them go, but they left him sweating with sudden apprehension.

They'd come from *above* him, between him and the cave! In the dusk, Hatchet must have infiltrated much deeper than he'd guessed when he heard that single, chopped-off sound of a whickering horse. Actually he had no way of knowing what might be happening up there. He knew only that, right now, he was in exactly the wrong place.

The pair looking for Sid Tacker was no problem for the moment. Leaving his hiding place. Bannister started to climb to the cave whose mouth showed a faint glimmer of light against the darker rimrock. At an instant his stretched nerves expected to hear an outcry, perhaps a scream from the woman or a burst of guns.

Coleman Dorsey knew the value of surprise. He sent Bob Ingram stumbling into the cave first, helpless in the grip of Russ Quint's meaty fist. Then, not giving time for a reaction, Dorsey himself ducked in under the low opening and let the people there see him, and see the glint of firelight on his revolver. He said sharply, "If you want to keep the kid alive, you'll drop your guns!"

No one moved from the positions in which he'd caught them; they gave back nothing but stares of utter bewilderment. But now young Ingram found his voice, half strangled by the hold Quint had on him. "Farley!" he cried. "I'm sorry! It's my fault. I walked right into them and let 'em jump me. I —"

"Shut up!" Quint ordered, and cuffed him to silence. His head rocked on his shoulders and his hat fell to the ground.

"The guns," Dorsey repeated.

"All right!" the older brother said

hoarsely. "Just don't hurt the boy!" He fumbled at his holster, drew the revolver from it and laid it on the stone floor. Willie Ryker hesitated, scowling in black fury, but a word from Ingram brought him under control. He plucked a long-barreled Colt from behind his waistband, and then watched sullenly as Dorsey moved forward and booted both weapons out of reach.

Dorsey looked next at the doctor. The latter, his face expressionless, simply lifted both skirts of his coat to show he was unarmed. Scarcely glancing at his wife, Dorsey now turned to Nat Hardman and leaned to snatch away the blanket that covered him to the chin. Satisfied it concealed nothing in the manner of a weapon, he nodded and let the blanket fall again. At his signal, Quint gave Bob Ingram a shove that dropped him to hands and knees and sent him scrambling to join the other prisoners.

Cole Dorsey looked them over, taking his time, studying their faces in the flickering light of the fire. Russ Quint demanded, "What about the big fellow? Where the hell's that range tramp?"

No one answered. Dorsey frowned over the question, and then shrugged. "He must be outside somewhere. The shooting we heard should have been him and Tacker having it out. Tell the boys to look till they find him. And to keep their eyes open. I'm taking no more chances with *that* one!"

As Quint passed the order to Nels McPhee and a couple of others who had been waiting at the mouth of the cave, Dorsey turned his attention to the smoke-blackened coffee pot. The aroma was tempting; his head, crudely bandaged, pounded with a fierce throb where the yellow-haired saddlebum had pistol-whipped him. Aggravated by hours in the saddle, the pain, at times, seemed enough to blind him and it had put him in a foul temper. He saw Doc Allen looking at him with narrow speculation, ignored him and instead told Farley Ingram, "Pour me a cup of that."

Wordlessly, the man obeyed. Letting Quint keep an eye and a gun on the prisoners, Dorsey took the cup and let himself down to the floor, leaning back as he sipped the hot brew and waited for the pounding to ease. Through a curtain of steam he watched a half dozen pairs of eyes peering silently at him.

The coffee did seem to help. He worked at it for a long moment without speaking, letting them wait. Abruptly he said, "Well, and what am I going to do about all this? You've put me to a damnable amount of bother."

"*We* have?" Farley Ingram exclaimed. And old Willie Ryker said hotly, "Who was it tried to seal off the hills? Who sent his hired guns to run Nat Hardman down and murder him?"

For their outburst Coleman Dorsey gave them no more than a cold and contemptuous look as he finished drinking. He said, "You got in my way. *All* of you! And I have too much at stake to allow that."

"You got nothing at stake!" old Hardman cried out in a shaking voice. He almost seemed about to try to climb up from the floor, except for his daughter's restraining hand. "You were nothing but an outsider, a nobody, without a dime, when I was fool enough to let you light!"

The pounding had started again, and the fury. Coleman Dorsey's fingers tightened on the empty cup as he made the effort that kept his voice steady. "You'd best watch your tongue," he snapped. "Old man, you're not going to cross me again!"

"I'll see you in hell," Nat Hardman cried, "before you get your way at Hatchet. If you think otherwise you're insane!"

All this time Sarah Dorsey, saying nothing, had been staring at her husband with eyes that took on a deeper and deeper tinge of dread. She said now, in a voice that didn't sound like hers, "Papa . . . I'm beginning to think he *is*."

The cup was flung aside and Dorsey was on his feet, in a single swift movement that ignored the sickening pain in his head. He stood over the woman and he shouted, *"Slut!"* After that he regained control again and watched her face turn white and heard the utter stillness about him.

He drew a shaking breath, and now his voice was very quiet, utterly reasonable. "I'm being generous," he told Nat Hardman. "I'm ready to give you your choice. What I want is a full partnership in Hatchet, and fifty-one percent controlling interest. Once the papers are drawn up and signed, as far as I'm concerned things can go back the way they were. We can forget all this."

"Forget?" Farley Ingram exclaimed. "Are you serious? What about *us?*"

"You don't concern me too much," Dorsey answered, with a shrug. "I can deal with you any time I feel like it — and Mort Woods, and all the others like you."

Doc Allen had been watching him all

this time with the same disturbing, professional stare. Now he said, "Man, have you forgotten there's a charge of attempted murder against you and your gunmen?"

"Show me your witness," Dorsey retorted. "Who's going to prefer charges, if Nat Hardman doesn't? And I'm certain he won't. Remember, I said I was giving him a choice."

"And what's the rest of it?" Hardman demanded in a hoarse voice.

"Why, you want to go on living, don't you? And you don't want anything happening to Sarah. But, it's up to you. The way things have worked out, it should be easy enough to make a clean sweep. Let the world think these Ingrams kidnapped you both in an attempt to force concessions, and when I tried to rescue, the whole lot of you were killed — not only you and the Ingrams, but your old friend the doctor who happened to get in the way. Now, do you really want to force my hand like that? Or will you listen to reason?"

Silently he added, *And stop this pounding in my head!* It was growing worse again and he knew why now, because all these people, who were at his mercy, insisted on crossing him. He wanted to shout at them that he would not be crossed!

Then the doctor was speaking again, calmly enough, and with that same clinical look in his eye. "It isn't going to work, you know. You can't just slaughter us all, out of hand, because you've forgotten one of your witnesses! What about the big fellow, that grubliner that's been the thorn in your hide from the start? You've let him get away from you again. And *he* knows the true story!"

"He won't live to tell it!" Dorsey answered, and felt his throat distend and knew he must indeed be shouting.

"I doubt that." Allen was still at it, picking at him with the quiet words. "*You're* the only one who isn't listening to reason. I think Nat was right! I really believe you're more than a little mad!"

Goaded beyond bearing, Coleman Dorsey took a stride toward the man and suddenly halted, as it came through to him that something was wrong. Allen was not really paying attention to him, nor were the others. All of them, all six of his hostages, were looking a little past him now, toward the entrance of the cave at his back. Half turning his head, he saw Russ Quint staring in the same direction.

And then he came clear around; and even as he saw the one who stood there he knew that all the talk had been simple treachery, distracting him, taking his attention, setting him up so that his nemesis could come at him unnoticed and without warning. . . .

Jim Bannister said sharply, "Don't use the gun!" but he knew he wasted his breath. Easing in from the darkness outside, he had managed to catch Russ Quint with his weapon in its holster; given another minute, he would have had the man disarmed and the rest should have been easy. But something must have alerted Coleman Dorsey to what was going on behind his back. Dorsey had turned, a mad recognition in his eyes. Bannister saw he was going to shoot, and he knew that to meet the threat meant releasing Quint, who would then be free to go for his own weapon.

The best chance was to get in first if possible, with a crippling shot at the hand that held Dorsey's sixgun, and hope to put him out of the fight in time to deal with Quint. But the pressures were too great and his move too hurried. A boot slipped on rock rubble and gave under him; his shot was jarred off just as he started down.

The bullet wasted itself against the rock floor of the cave, and screamed off in ricochet. But the stumble probably saved his life from the bullet Russ Quint flung at him, to lose itself past his shoulder somewhere in the outer darkness.

On his knee, Bannister thumbed back the hammer of his own gun and found himself staring past the muzzle of Coleman Dorsey's weapon, into mad eyes in a face turned livid with fury. The moment seemed interminable; then they both fired, together. Muzzle flame seared his vision as the blasting of the guns, within that narrow and reverberating space, shocked his eardrums. But he felt no impact, sensed that Dorsey had misjudged the target made by a man kneeling in front of him, while for Bannister himself it would have been impossible to miss.

His bullet took Dorsey in the chest, and the man took a step backward and went down.

Desperately aware of Russ Quint, at the edge of his vision, Bannister jerked around, hunting for him through the burning sting of smoke. He could only blink at what he saw, his mind and senses numbed by the battering punishment of concussion. Had there been a third shot? For Russ Quint had slammed back against the rock wall; he had dropped his gun and now, slowly, he was bending forward and crumpling in his tracks. Suddenly he broke and pitched onto his face; and that was when Bannister saw Doc Allen on his knees, with one hand holding open his leather medical bag. A snubnosed pistol was in the other hand, smoke trailing from its muzzle. The doctor was watching Russ Quint to make sure the one bullet had been enough.

Reaction hit Bannister and his legs shook under him as he got onto his feet. His glance fell upon Sarah Dorsey. She had both hands pressed against her mouth, her eyes enormous and dark in a face completely drained of color.

Then, remembering they weren't yet out of danger, he turned and ducked through the entrance, moving quickly to keep from silhouetting himself against the glow of the fire. He put his back to the rock and listened to the night stillness through the ringing that filled his ears.

He could only guess how many of their crew Dorsey and Quint had brought with them. Sid Tacker, for one, he knew was dead, and he knew that another probably remained where a chop of Bannister's gun-barrel had dropped him without sound, when they nearly collided a moment ago in the dark below the cave. But the rest would have heard the stuttering exchange of gunfire and they were probably wondering what it meant, and perhaps waiting for someone to give them further orders.

Impatient, Bannister decided to set them straight. "Hatchet!" he shouted, and his voice bounced echoes off the rimrock that rose behind him. "Coleman Dorsey is dead. So is Quint. It leaves nobody to pay your wages. But if you want to make a fight of it, there's five guns up here ready to oblige you!"

Silence, then, except for the strengthening night wind sweeping through the trees and along the rimrock. Someone stepped out beside him. It was Farley Ingram, carrying a gun. Together they studied the tangled blackness, and suddenly Farley said between his teeth, "Listen!"

"I hear it," Bannister said.

Somewhere below them a horse had started into motion. It was joined by a second, and then by several at once, the spatter of hoof-beats sounding clearly. They beat up a quick crescendo that as quickly faded out, to be echoed briefly a moment later as they struck some patch of hardrock and then crossing that, could be heard no more.

Farley Ingram let out his breath. "Do you suppose that's the end of it?"

"We can hope so."

Bannister slid his gun into the holster and turned to re-enter the cave. Ingram followed him in.

Not much had changed. The woman, recovering from the first shock, had her face buried against her father's shoulder and was weeping, with his arm around her to comfort her as best he could. Doc Allen was just straightening from examining the men who had been shot, and his nod told Bannister that both were dead. "We'd better get these outside," he said crisply. "We don't need them in here!"

Ingram signaled his brother and Willie Ryker; as they came to help, he said, "And after that we'll scout around a little, just to make sure."

Jim Bannister left the job to them. The doctor was building up the fire with sticks of dry wood. Watching him, Bannister said, "I'm curious. Do you always carry a gun in that bag of yours?"

"In this kind of country," the other said, "it pays to play safe."

"A lucky thing Cole Dorsey never thought to check!" He added, lowering his voice, "What about the woman? She's been

248

put through a lot — partly by me, I'm sorry to say."

Allen shook his head. "She and Nat both had to learn the truth, that the man she married was plain crazy! But she comes of tough stock, she'll get through this. Let her cry it out awhile. Then, if she needs it, I can give her something to help her sleep."

"Here?" Dubiously, Bannister looked about them.

"Why not? We can make her comfortable enough. Then, come morning we can think about your suggestion of moving Nat over the old trail to Wolford's. It shouldn't be too much of a job. In fact," and he looked squarely at Bannister, "we should be able to handle it without you. If you feel like you want to leave. . . ."

A cold knot formed in Bannister's middle, as he looked into the man's shrewd eyes and wondered what was behind them and how much of the truth about him those eyes might have fathomed. Allen returned his look coolly, without a twitch of expression in his bearded face; if he really knew the tall drifter's secret, something suggested it would be safe with him.

Then the question from Nat Hardman spared Bannister the need of a reply.

"Bonner? What's this talk of leaving?"

Hardman was frowning at him; the woman too, was sitting up and mopping her face with her neckcloth, looking at him in concern. "You said you won't take pay for what you've done," the rancher said gruffly, "but by God, there's certainly a job for you at Hatchet as long as you want it. You name your own salary!"

Bannister hesitated a long minute, while dry wood crackled in the fire and these people waited to hear his answer, even the doctor, with that skeptical, knowing look that seemed to know perfectly well what the answer would have to be. It was a temptation to accept. This was a remote country, and now it would be a friendly one. A man grew deathly weary of forever traveling, with his attention as much on the back trail as on what might lie ahead. Yet the back trail was always there, and with the price Jim Bannister carried as bait, there could never be any knowing what might be following behind him, perhaps no more than hours away. . . .

Regretfully, he shook his head. "I appreciate the offer," he told Nat Hardman. "But I know it wouldn't work. I'd soon be drifting again — it's hard for a fiddlefoot to light anywhere." *Or a man outside the law,* he might have added. For either, it was a bleak way of life.

Hardman and his daughter, at least, simply could not understand. The rancher shook his head in puzzlement. "But, *why?*"

Bannister pretended not to hear. "Guess I'll have to look around, see if there's anything else needs to be done. Otherwise I'll probably be riding come daylight."

And he turned and went out of there into the chill dark where the stars now were a glittering mesh above the shouldering peaks and where he would have no more questions to answer, nor have to meet the speculations he knew would lie in the doctor's shrewd and searching gaze.

We hope you have enjoyed this Large Print book. Other Thorndike, Wheeler or Chivers Press Large Print books are available at your library or directly from the publishers.

For more information about current and upcoming titles, please call or write, without obligation, to:

Publisher
Thorndike Press
295 Kennedy Memorial Drive
Waterville, ME   04901
Tel. (800) 223-1244

Or visit our Web site at:
www.gale.com/thorndike
www.gale.com/wheeler

OR

Chivers Large Print
published by BBC Audiobooks Ltd
St James House, The Square
Lower Bristol Road
Bath BA2 3SB
England
Tel. +44(0) 800 136919
email: bbcaudiobooks@bbc.co.uk
www.bbcaudiobooks.co.uk

All our Large Print titles are designed for easy reading, and all our books are made to last.